D0425260

deadville

deadville

RON KOERTGE

CANDLEWICK PRESS
CAMBRIDGE, MASSACHUSETTS

Copyright © 2008 by Ron Koertge

First edition 2008

Library of Congress Cataloging-in-Publication Data is available.

Library of Congress Cataloging Card Number 2008025448

ISBN 978-0-7636-3580-0

2 4 6 8 10 9 7 5 3 1

Printed in the United States of America

This book was typeset in Bembo.

Candlewick Press
2067 Massachusetts Avenue
Cambridge, Massachusetts 02140

visit us at www.candlewick.com

Thanks

to Bianca and Jan, Kaylan, Katie, and Liz,
whose sharp eyes brought this ship safely home.

ONE

I'm washing my hands in the bathroom a couple of doors down from the principal's office. Washing and rinsing. Soaping up again. Washing and rinsing.

"Hey, Ryan."

In the mirror it's Tim Boynton, a guy I used to play soccer with. I nod at his reflection.

"Anything goin' on?" He's grinning big.

I tell him, "Ask Andy."

He flashes a couple of bills. "I'm asking you. Just a couple of joy sticks."

"I don't deal, Tim."

"You did a couple of weeks ago."

"It was a favor to Andy, all right? A onetime thing."

"So where's Andy?"

I hit the little button on the soap dispenser and start in one last time. "Dunno."

Tim puts the money away. Now he's disgruntled. "Well, tell him I'm looking for him."

I turn on the hot water and watch my hands wrestle with each other.

I run into Andy right after sixth period. "Tim Boynton's looking for you."

He gets me by the arm. "Took care of him in gym. C'mon. We're going to Saint Mary's. Charlotte Silano fell off her horse."

Andy scatters some ninth-graders who are jammed up at the bottom of the big concrete stairs. First of all, he's a senior. Second of all, he's huge. Or maybe it's just that he's huge. Anyway, they scatter.

I tell him, "Somebody said she broke her leg."

"Or her neck," he says. "Or is unconscious or, like, dead."

"She's not dead. If she was dead, there'd be an announcement. And not to sound too callous, but what do you care, anyway?"

"Are you kidding? She bankrolled a party every couple of weeks. My PR people tell me customers appreciate the human touch. Christmas cards, 'how's the wife and kids,' a firm handshake. That kind of thing. So we'll go by, and I'll say how sorry I am to hear about her unfortunate accident. That way she'll remember me the next time her and her friends get together to count their money."

"I don't like hospitals."

He opens the door to his old Toyota, the only car in the lot with duct tape holding on its back bumper. "Five minutes away."

I stop with my hand on the corroded handle. "And I really don't want to go to Saint Mary's."

He gets in, starts the car, then pats the dash like it's the flank of a big animal. "Keep me company. Wait in the lot if you want. I'll be like three minutes. Then I'll take you home."

I look toward the street, where about nine thousand kids are waiting. Andy knows what I'm thinking.

"Forget the stupid bus." He takes a spliff out of his shirt pocket, the place anyone else would carry a gel pen. "Look what I've got." His voice is teasing, playful, and insinuating. I feel like I ought to say, "My, what big teeth you have."

When we get in the car, I reach for the weed, glance around to see if anybody's looking (anybody with a badge), then light it and take a hit. "Okay, but I'm waiting outside."

"Fine. You can guard the car. This baby's worth a fortune in Bangladesh."

We're easing out of the lot when Chris Teagarden backs out right in front of us in his red Mustang. Andy has to hit the brakes, and I reach for the dash to brace myself. I've got the seat belt on, but it just hangs there like a sash. Chris gives us the finger like the almost accident was our fault, then patches out.

Andy has both arms around the steering wheel, and he's leaning his chin on his right hand. He looks almost thoughtful. "I hate that guy," he says calmly.

I reach into my backpack for my player, put the little earplugs in, and lean back. The window on my side is permanently down, so there's always a breeze in Andy's car. To my right is the long, roiled-up lawn of LBJ High. It's a big, old-fashioned building with pillars in front and stone lions that flank the main steps. The stoned lions, as they are popularly known, because of their sleepy, semi-blissful expressions. Inside, the ceilings are very high, like students fifty years ago were lanky with long necks and legs. Now we're short with metal in our tongues and ears.

A bunch of ninth-graders plunge through the cross-walk. They've all got small faces, and most of them are still wearing clothes their mothers insist on. A couple of the boys are holding basketballs like mementos of the French Revolution. To make that image complete, one of them has drawn droopy eyes and a frowny face on his Rawlings Special.

We take Foothill Boulevard to the hospital. It's maybe ten blocks.

I sing along with the Killers' "For Reasons Unknown" and let the dope run its hand down my ruffled fur.

"Hey, man, you asleep?"

I shake my head. "I'm fine."

"Senior history's driving me nuts. What the hell's the cold war?"

I sit up a little. "About fifty years' worth of trash talk between the U.S. and the USSR. They were our allies during World War II, and then they got all feisty. When's your paper due?"

Andy glides over into the right lane. "You're so suspicious."

"When's it due, Andy?"

At the stoplight we're idling next to a black Maxima. The driver is this thirty-something lady who's really put together: hair, eyes, jewelry. Everything matches everything else. Long dark hair like Charlotte Silano. Skin like hers. Charlotte Silano all grown-up.

Andy says, "Like next week."

I ask, "How many pages?"

"Four to six."

"I can handle that."

He reaches across and into the glove compartment, an easy move because the little door is somewhere in the backseat. He shows me a tightly wound joint. "Maui Wauie," he says. "You know how regular weed gives you the munchies for chocolate? The guy I got it from claims you smoke a little of this and you want pineapple and poo."

"Poi."

He nods. "I knew that sounded wrong."

We pull into the parking lot of the hospital. The place is huge, almost like a city in one of those old sci-fi novels, especially the catwalks between the towers. Andy points to a big banner draped across a brand-new wing: WE REALLY CARE.

I tell him, "I feel better already."

He parks in the red zone and climbs out. "Sure you don't want to come? I know what you're thinking. This is not that, okay? It's a whole different scene."

I take a deep breath. "Maybe you're right."

But when we start to go through those big automatic doors that open into the lobby, I can't seem to move.

"C'mon," says Andy.

"I think I changed my mind."

He shoves me. "Will you get inside?"

Those big couches are still huddled around giant coffee tables. And two volunteers who'd retired from their real lives run the information desk. They probably aren't the same women, but they look the same. They have the same green jumpers over their regular clothes. I think about that: Is green a comforting color? Does it always mean "It's safe to go"? Their purses are identical, too—pretend leather with stiff handles. They flank the PC console. I can imagine these ladies at the end of the day picking up their handbags and waltzing right out of here. Not a care in the world.

Andy leans on the counter. "Silano, Charlotte. She's new."

One of them taps her computer a few times. "Your friend is in the ICU, on the seventh floor."

"They probably won't let you see her," says the other.

Someone's coming out of the gift shop with an "It's a Girl" balloon, and there's that funeral-home smell from the flowers.

"Actually, we'll just go up and check things out," says Andy. "Maybe she's better." He gets me by the arm. "We'll find out what's up and then we're done."

He's dragging me toward the elevator, where three kids from Charlotte's class are waiting (it's also Andy's class, but these guys are a whole other species). Kevin Gibson—a wide receiver with a scholarship to UCLA and LBJ High's answer to Tiger Woods if Tiger Woods played football—holds this giant "Get Well" card covered with signatures. A horse on the front looks depressed. "I'm Sorry" floats in a speech balloon. Chloe Carter is still in her song girl outfit. From outside comes the wail of a siren, like a big, red, wagging tongue. I hold the door for everybody and then push eight like I used to.

"Seven, stupid. The ICU's on seven." Chloe looks me over and then kind of turns away like I smell bad.

Andy tells her, "We'll sign that card."

"It's for Charlotte."

"Yeah, I know," he says. "That's why we want to sign it."

"Okay, I guess." She doesn't move, but she does look at Kevin. She wants him to intervene. He's staring at the ceiling with his eyes rolled up like somebody in an Annunciation painting. When she finally holds the pen out to Andy, he shakes his head.

"Actually," he says, "I'll tell her in person."

Chloe just looks at him.

"She's alive, right?" Andy says.

"She's unconscious." Chloe looks at her friends and mutters, "Who let these losers in?"

The elevator door opens right into the ICU waiting room. It's not the same wing Molly was in, but there are the same orange couches and chairs and a little table full of old magazines. The same big glass windows and, behind those, the same half-dozen beds with curtains between them. Equipment everywhere that blinks and registers and reads out. What do they do with the reams of paper left over after people die? The doctors pored over them and faxed them and made copies, then called relatives into their offices so they could sit in those bad-news chairs and nod.

But in this waiting room, there are a half a dozen kids from school standing around. The girls hang on each other. The boys stare at the floor.

I tell myself that Andy's right. This is a whole different scene.

"How is she?" Chloe asks.

Nan Winter shrugs and pulls at her miniskirt.

Chloe marches to the desk, leans toward the nurse bent over a computer, and starts grilling her. Everybody else—Diamande Glass, Brad Cary, Elena Burnham, and Charlotte's boyfriend, Derek Shaddow—stares at Andy and me. Jill Warner, who looks stoned out of her mind, is propped up against the wall. Andy and I go stand by her: birds of a feather.

Brad walks right up to us. He's a senior who likes to stroll around the locker room naked and spit mouthfuls of water on anybody who dresses in a hurry. "Hey, Andy," he says. "I was lookin' for you."

"Yeah?"

"Let's step outside."

That leaves me all alone with the ruling class: Diamande, Elena, Derek, and Jill. Don't their names just say it all: swimming pools and BMWs on their sixteenth birthdays. Betty Bennett, a girl I've known since kindergarten, is kind of off by herself.

I know a few things about nurses—you don't get anywhere giving them attitude. I watch Betty go up to the same one Chloe recently interrogated to no avail.

"This is probably a stupid question," Betty says, "but the faster Charlotte comes out of this, the better, right?"

"Of course," the nurse says.

"And there's no way of knowing when she—"

A head shake cuts her off. "We're going to take real good care of her."

"I know. I just, you know, wondered." Then she steps away.

Diamande stops her. "What'd she say?"

"Not much." And Betty comes over and leans between Jill and me.

I feel like I ought to say something, so I try, "I didn't know you and Charlotte were friends."

"We're not. We play volleyball together." Betty laces her fingers together and holds both arms out, making a narrow V. "I set it up, and she drives it down their throats. I didn't come with these guys or anything." We're about the same height, so she looks right at me. "How about you?"

"How about me what?"

"How do you know Charlotte?"

"Oh, I don't really. I came with Andy."

Betty looks at her nails. They're painted a mysterious green, not like shutters or vegetables. More like underwater. "Andy Rey," she says, "teen entrepreneur. If he wasn't selling weed, he could be Mr. Junior Achievement." She looks right at my T-shirt. "Brutal Noodle?"

"It's a band, not a special at the Olive Garden."

Just then this couple comes in and the others surround them. Charlotte's parents, for sure. A fit-looking guy with his head shaved, and his pretty wife in a kind of parrot-colored outfit (red top, green pants). In this environment it seems way out of place.

Andy's hand falls on my shoulder. "You ready, man?"

I take a last look through the window at Charlotte in her cubicle. Why is it so dim? It's not like a lot of light is going to wake her up.

We're going down in the elevator when I ask Andy, "You sold Brad dope?"

He leans back against the fake-grain wall. "So?"

"He's an asshole."

"A nickel bag is all."

"And that makes it all right?"

"I'm an equal-opportunity vendor, okay?"

On the main floor, he holds the door so somebody pushing an empty wheelchair can get on. Then he lets me slide out. Different-colored footprints go off in all directions—X-Ray, Hematology, Oncology. We follow the red ones to the lobby.

"You did okay up there," he says. "You totally coped."

Outside I take a deep breath and look around. Something's wrong with the hospital's sprinkler system. There are evenly spaced depressions in the grass every half-dozen yards, like a giant's footprints. "Let's go to your house."

"Absolutely."

We step aside so a family can get by on their way to the parking lot. The mother and both her daughters are wearing bunched-up shawls that look like seaweed. And the little boy, maybe six years old, is dragging a toy shovel. The sound of the aluminum blade on concrete makes my heart wobble.

I look at Andy. He's big and warm and smells kind of sour. He's always got something stupid on his T-shirt. This one says TODAY'S THE DAY THE TEDDY BEARS HAVE THEIR PICNIC.

I tap the word TEDDY and say, "Your mom buy that for you?"

"Hey, man. I've got a teddy bear T-shirt for every day of the week." Then he opens the car door for me.

Andy's house is always hot. Maybe it's the oven; maybe it's just that it's little and five people live there. Five pretty large people.

When we walk in, nobody even looks up. Andy's dad will bet on anything, so he's got horse racing on the big TV and baseball on the little one. I'd have to have smoke coming out of my pants before he'd notice me.

Mrs. Rey is tapping away on her computer, but Andy's little brothers—Otto and Art—stop playing Twenty Questions and Battleship long enough to say hi. Both of them look radioactive from Cheetos dust.

"Mom got these games for us," says Otto.

I pretend to look. "Cool."

"We play with 'em, then she sells 'em back and gets us new ones." Art makes me hold one and it's sticky. "Want to play?"

"Leave Ryan alone," says Andy. "A friend of ours just fell off a horse."

"Is the horse okay?" asks Otto.

I hand back the sticky game. "Yeah, and he's sorry."

Andy pulls me toward the kitchen, and to get there we have to thread our way through piles of stuff: dolls in plastic cases, stacks of sheet music, cowboy boots, a couple of quilts, and digital pics of all kinds of things—a chandelier, a weather vane, and a porthole.

"Where's the rest of the ship?" I ask Andy.

"Don't ask. It's probably on the FedEx truck."

His mom scoots back from the computer and coasts toward the dining room. She's wearing a shimmery-looking muumuu that hangs down to the floor, so it's like watching a big jellyfish.

She holds up a little stuffed bear. "Annette Funicello," she says. "Bought it for nine; now it's worth fifty. It goes out today." She points to that popcorn packing stuff that's pretty much everywhere and then to a pile of boxes. "You want anything, Ryan?" She takes a cookie off a Tower of Pisa–size stack right beside her computer. "Try one of these."

"That Emeril guy will be here any minute, Mom. Let's don't spoil Ryan's dinner."

Andy leads me into the kitchen. He's got the freezer open, and he's holding half a dozen frozen dinners.

"I've got Calypso Coconut Shrimp; I've got Poppers and Hot Pockets. But for my money, it's the Hungry-Man series." He tosses them out, like big playing cards. "All Day Breakfast, Roasted Carved Turkey Breast, Angus Beef Meatloaf. Ready in a jiffy."

I take a deep breath. "Sure, why not. You pick for me."

While the dinners are nuking, Andy opens a beer, chugs about half of it, belches prodigiously, and hands me the rest.

He's grinning and that's a welcome sight. In the other room, his dad's yelling at a horse. His mom's selling bears on the Internet. Otto and Art are fighting as they work their way through a six-pack of cupcakes. It was way too quiet in that hospital.

I watch Andy wash a couple of forks, then slide the dinners onto the table. He butters a piece of bread. It's not whole wheat, but it isn't white, either. It seems to resist the butter, too; no matter how hard Andy presses down with his knife. Stubborn bread.

Eventually he leans into his food, and when he's done, he reaches for what's left of mine.

I let him and then say, "My dad chews everything he eats thirty-two times."

"Your dad chews his Angus Beef Meatloaf thirty-two times? Good for him." He stands up. "C'mon, let's have some fun. First we wash the car, then we mow the lawn, then we separate paper and plastic, and then we do our homework."

We're walking past the washer and dryer on his back porch when he throws one arm over my shoulder, grins, and says, "Thirty-two times. You crack me up."

The backyard is like an obstacle course—pink flamingos, garden angels, turtles, and bearded gnomes with red pointy hats.

I point. "EBay?"

Andy nods and lets his hand fall right on the nearest little statue. "This is Sloppy, and over there's Droopy and Pervo and Tithead and—"

I hold up one hand. "I get the picture."

"I can never remember the other three, anyway," he

says. He points up into this ancient elm tree, and there's what's left of a tree house. No walls and no roof. It's a raft. A deck. A platform. A leftover from some flood. Maybe the Flood.

The rungs—that word should have those ironic quote marks around it—nailed into the tree all point in different directions like twenty-five-cent compasses. When Andy starts to climb, I get out of the way. I don't want to be underneath if he has a great fall.

It must be all those dwarfs that make me start thinking about Charlotte Silano laid out in a long glass coffin.

Andy shouts down at me. "Hey! You comin' or not?"

I take my time. It's a gorgeous old tree, with a beauty that kind of hurts. But it's a harmless hurt. And it approves of everything. Even what I'm about to do.

By the time I'm pulling myself up and over, Andy's already got his special mahogany carrying case open and out comes his favorite glass water pipe. He opens an Evian bottle and starts to pack in some herb. Then he hands me a yellow Bic lighter and the pipe.

"Is this new?" I ask, tapping on the glass.

He shakes his head.

"It's spotless."

"A craftsman takes care of his tools."

He watches me inhale and lie back. Andy always

has good stuff. A couple of hits, and the leaves have this way about them. All of a sudden, I'd like to listen to this album called *Farewell to the Shade* by AATT. The whole name is And Also the Trees, but I like AATT. There're very mystical cats, almost pagan. They're also famous in the best way, that is, not everybody knows who they are.

Andy blurts, "Who were those little suckers, anyway?"

I know what he means. My sister, Molly, and I were like that. We knew what the other one was thinking.

I recite, "Sneezy, Sleepy, Dopey, Doc, Happy, Grumpy, Bashful."

He's holding in the smoke, so he gives me the "Say again?" look.

So I say it again. "Sneezy, Sleepy, Dopey, Doc, Happy, Grumpy, Bashful."

He takes another hit, twice as hearty as any of mine. "How do you do that?"

"It's a trick. Two S's, two D's, and three emotions."

He exhales and there's a kind of ominous rumble deep in his body. Andy coughs all winter, and the warm weather only helps a little. "But there's more than three emotions," he says. "What about Depressed?"

I picture a runt with a long face. "There just wouldn't be a dwarf named Depressed. He'd be the outcast of the gift shop."

"And what's with the two S's? There are tons of S's—Stupid, Sleazy, Spike . . ." He gropes around in his brain. "Snorkel."

The weed is strong, and Andy likes to, as they say in the business, get lifted fast. And he's not exactly alone. I can feel the merriment building and I'm grateful. Ganja as pacifier. Ask your friendly pharmacist. I say, "Leaving aside for the moment Sleazy and Stupid, why would there be a dwarf named Spike?"

"He's the kick-ass dwarf. Butt you right in the balls with his little pointy hat. The prince shows up, that faggot, and Spike says, 'Get your mitts off those knockers, pal. Those are ours.'"

I'm two people now. One who knows this isn't really funny, and one who thinks it's hilarious. The accuser and the stoner.

The latter asks, "And Snorkel?"

Andy squirms. "Like, you know, Snorkel's the aquadwarf. For when the mine floods or they go to Cancun for some R & R."

I picture the little red hats and the beards and the shovels and the lanterns and the Speedos and the air tank on Snorkel's back and a beach in Mexico. It's the best I've felt all day.

I start thinking about this weird novel I read out loud to Molly when she was in the hospital the first time. There were all these multiple universes, so many that somebody could go to an empty one and be like a king. Make all the rules, do anything he wanted. Decide who got in and who didn't. What got in and what didn't. Like sadness would be banned. If anybody wanted a little dose of that, he could go to Sadland for the weekend.

Eventually I scoot to the edge of the tree house and let my legs dangle over the side. All I need is a fishing pole and the Mississippi. I'm the new Huck Finn. I light out for the territory by lighting up.

Andy kind of oozes up beside me and holds out the pipe.

I shake my head. "I have to be able to sit up straight at dinner."

He inhales, then leans into me so hard, at first I think maybe he's passing out. But he's just screwing around. Next he punches me in the shoulder, so I punch him back. Then he holds out one hand, and we thumb-wrestle or at least spar. Finally he flips me off and then gives me the rocker's salute—the index finger and pinkie fingers straight up with everything else tucked in.

I say, *"Mano cornuta,"* with all the Italian I can muster from my mother's side of the family.

"Who's the guy who invented that?" Andy asks.

"The devil's horns? It's, like, folklore. To ward off the evil eye."

He shakes his head. "No, no. That KISS guy. The one who had the cow's tongue transplanted in his mouth."

I take two Oreos out of his chocolate stash. And actually they're not Oreos. They're knock-offs, but I've got the munchies.

I say, "You're talking about Gene Simmons, and that's actually his tongue."

"No way."

"His real name is Chaim Witz."

"Bullshit."

I shake my head at the bong again. "What'd you think—that he was born wearing bat-wing makeup and dragon boots? He taught school right out of college, and he speaks about five languages. But he loved rock 'n' roll so much, he started a band named Rainbow. He was Gene Klein then."

"Then who's Gene Simmons?"

"Same guy, just pre-KISS."

"How do you know this stuff?"

"I read."

"Yeah, but then you remember it."

I hold up my arms and pretend to cower. "Don't beat me, Pa. It won't happen again."

Off to the west, the sky looks tired. I know I have to go home pretty soon. Charlotte Silano's in her room, a room so white she could be lost in a snowstorm, the kind where anybody might lie down and that's that.

Did you just want to stretch out and catch forty winks? Don't give in. Nothing's broken. You're not even bruised. Grab hold of your bootstraps and pull! Want to sing along while you do that? Here's Britt Daniel and Spoon—"Waiting for the Kid to Come Out."

I say, "Those guys get on my nerves."

"Which guys?" Andy uncrosses his legs and lets them dangle over the edge. His cutoffs are frayed, but not like the ones at Abercrombie. And the stains aren't from playing lacrosse.

"Charlotte's friends. Jill, Brad, Derek. Those guys."

"Be careful, dude. You could've been them."

"Shut up."

He shrugs. "Your folks knew their folks. You played sports and you were good. You could be going with some chick like Charlotte Silano."

I pat him on the shoulder. "I gotta get out of here."

He struggles trying to get to his feet. Sitting like we were, a lot of blood ran to his ankles, which are still bright red. And he hasn't exactly got ankles, anyway. Just calves that go right into his high-tops.

I steady him. "You'll fall out of here if you're not careful."

He waves me away. "I fall out of here all the time. Stand back."

He actually does pretty well. One rung after another. At the bottom he looks up, opens his arms, and recites, "Romeo, Romeo. Where the hell are you?"

TWO

Third period. A couple of minutes before math. I lean on the wall outside and close my eyes: *Mr. Birney, the pi man, will bring his usual glacial pace to class today, so let's all greet him with robotic stares. And by the way, the tenth-grade replicants are in the shop for rewiring, so if one of them was doing your homework, I'd check it first. Now from the home for the criminally insane, also known as LBJ High, let's start this set with Pink Floyd and the obvious but nonetheless rousing "Another Brick in the Wall."*

My sister loved it when I did that stuff.

The bell rings. I hold the door for a couple of girls (they don't even look at me, the Phantom Doorman), then I take a quiz off the corner of the desk and glance at it:

Compute the value of
$\sin(5 \pi/12) = \sin(\pi/4 + \pi/6)$
Use the sum formula for the sine function.

Find the value of the infinite sum
$1 + 1/2 + 1/4 + \ldots + 1/2^n + \ldots$
Use the geometric series formula.

I make my way to the back of the room, past the chairs with the wraparound desks for all the right-handed people. Andy squeezed into one once and couldn't get out. When he stood up, he was like some kind of cyborg— half boy, half furniture.

So I settle at a table with a girl named Allyssa Pomerance, who's back there because she's a lefty, too. Word is she lives in the basement of her house, back in what was supposed to be a wine cellar maybe or even a bomb shelter but is now just a kind of cave. For somebody who is reputed to thrive on subterranean darkness, her skin always gives off a weird kind of light. I hang my Guns N' Roses hoodie over the back of the chair.

"Hey, Ryan," Allyssa says. "Have you seen those drawings of mammoths all over town?"

"Not yet."

"They're all over town. What do you think they mean? Is it like those THE END IS NEAR signs?"

I shrug and fiddle with my iPod, running through an anthology of album covers. I even hold it up so she can see: *Stories from the City, Strangeways, Here We Come, Placebo, Exciter.*

"Well, it's got to mean something," she says. "Do you think maybe Charlotte was the first victim? The whole thing creeps me out."

"Charlotte fell off a horse, not a mammoth."

She aims her tiny alabaster nose at me. "You could wear cooler shirts if you wanted to. You've still kind of got a nice body."

"Ladies and gentlemen." Mr. Birney taps on his desk with a red Bic. "Quizzes facedown, please. All electronic devices off."

Allyssa rolls her eyes. "We've only been staring at them for five minutes."

"Miss Pomerance?"

"Just talking about the weather, sir."

There's snow in the foothills, and every flake's the same. And now here's "When We Turned the Corner, She Was Gone," by Mad 4 Plaid.

"You may begin now."

I look at the fluorescent lights as if I'm at the beach, arching my back a little and giving my face up to the glare. I can smell the wax and the buffing compound the janitors use. Mr. Birney drifts around the room. He's almost bald, but he's still got this pathetic ponytail. My hair is black and kind of curly. I bet he would kill for my hair.

Unlike the rogue's gallery of poets in English and everything but a bottle of wine and a mime in French class, Mr. Birney's only got one thing in his classroom—a big picture of a nautilus shell. He uses it to talk about Fibonacci numbers: 1, 1, 2, 3, 5, 8, 13, et cetera. Two and three are five, five and eight are thirteen, and so on. Which is, according to Mr. Birney, beautiful. Which they kind of are. They're something you can depend on, anyway. And they don't make anybody think it's dangerous just to be alive.

"Let's do the first problem," says Mr. Birney. "Who'll go to the board for me? Ryan?"

"I didn't finish."

"Your father would be proud. Somebody else?"

I feel like a movie that's slid off the screen and is wobbling around in midair. Like it's showing itself on the impurities in the atmosphere. I can see the movie, and I'm in it. I can put my hand through it, but it's real, too.

The bell rings, and I head for the cafeteria to meet Andy. Jill Warner and Diamande Glass blast out of the girls' bathroom, cutting me off like they're sports cars and I'm a bread truck. They rendezvous with two more of Charlotte Silano's friends, hug each other without messing up their hair, then blow their perfect noses. Diamande is

26

wearing her boots and those half-tight/half-loose riding pants. She and Charlotte used to ride together.

The cafeteria's double doors swing open. My mom would take one look at those steam tables and just shake her head. She thinks it's a crime to mistreat food. I shuffle along behind a cut-rate hobbit and a couple of air-guitar gods with Rod Stewart hair who can't decide between something that smells like eucalyptus or a naked burger patty that looks like it was run over.

A lady who was probably born wearing a hairnet asks me, "What'll it be, honey?"

"Got any giraffe?"

She gives me the look she's given a thousand other wise guys.

I say, "Then any mass of cells will do."

I give the cashier the twenty Mom left on my dresser.

When I get to the table, there's Andy with two of everything. He moves a plate, slides a saucer, tips an empty milk carton on its side. It's like chess in a way. Cannibal chess. He gobbles up the losers.

I sit across from him, my back to the room. This is our table. We're like math geeks, gear heads, and techies. Except we're a clique of two.

I tell him, "Allyssa Pomerance said I still have kind of a nice body."

He doesn't even look up. "'Still' and 'kind of.'"

"I've already noted the qualifiers."

"Like she knows anything. She eats tofu." Then he points behind me with his fork. "Check this out."

It's Eddie Tanaka again. Eddie with the glasses, Eddie with the meds and the inhaler, Eddie the super-loser. Eddie who scurries. But not fast enough.

Chris Teagarden and his gang are all over him. Apparently they're back from prowling the noxious fogs of the lowlands. They strip off his backpack and start tossing it around. Eddie runs back and forth like a lab rat. Other kids laugh or look away.

Andy puts down his fork. "Damnit, I'm tryin' to eat."

When he gets up, I get up, too. We walk over. I grab the backpack out of the air, hand it to Eddie, and say, "You're okay."

Chris—always in a muscle shirt even when it's so cold his actually fairly skinny arms get all goose-bumpy—snarls, "Stay out of this, Glazier."

"Now, now." I like to fight. Then I don't feel so much like a ghost. But I don't bother with all the preening and caterwauling.

He looks at his cronies. When he shoves me, I'm ready for him.

But just before he can do anything, Mr. Roberts steps between us.

"What's the problem, gentlemen?"

Out the window I can see one of those shiny catering trucks. Not the kind that go to people's houses, but the kind that drive around and stop at construction sites and places like that. They're beautiful in a way, dimpled and shiny. I could do that. Drive a shiny truck, wash it on the weekends, make change, and hand people food.

Chris shakes his head. "I don't see any problem."

Mr. Roberts just sighs. "Try to keep a lid on it, okay?"

I settle down in front of my tray again and take a deep breath. Andy starts eating right where he left off. His plate looks like a construction site.

"We should be goons," he says between bites. "Go to the East Coast and work for the Mob. Wear black suits, drive big black cars. There's these girls who are like Mafia groupies. They bring you cannelloni and pizza and espresso anytime you want."

"Those are waitresses."

"Then they start kissing on you."

Three jocks drift our way. They're seniors like Andy. Football has been over for months, but they still go by their last names, just like their jerseys said. Used to say. Lehane, Derricotte, Johnston. They were linemen, so they're big, but not big like Andy.

"I'd like to really take care of Teagarden," Lehane says. "He's too pretty. I feel like moving his nose around."

"You seen his slingshot?" Johnston asks. "He's got this,

like, hunter's slingshot. Shoots ball bearings. That guy. I'd like to wrap that thing around his neck."

Derricotte chimes in, "He's gonna end up in juvie. Then he'll be sorry. Lots of guys tougher than him down there."

Lehane looks down at Andy. "You gonna do that thing we talked about? You could win, man."

"I might," Andy says. He reaches for his desserts.

"Who's the guy he has to beat, Ryan?"

"Don't look at me."

"Joey Chestnut," says Andy. "He ate sixty-six hot dogs in twelve minutes. Buns, too."

"You could do that, Andy," Derricotte says. "You totally could. You can eat, man. I know because I can eat, but no way am I in your league. You gotta go to New York and compete."

I've heard this conversation before, so my mind wanders. I kind of miss Charlotte Silano flitting around in those riding pants. She was incredibly good-looking, and now she's laid out in that hospital room. It's true what I told Betty, that I really didn't know her at all. But now I almost can't stop thinking about her.

"Maybe I'll meet Sonya Thomas," says Andy. "A few years ago she put away forty-six oysters in ten minutes. Eleven pounds of cheesecake in nine. Didn't puke, either. Girl of my dreams."

All three of them laugh and move on, bouncing off each other like electrons.

"They're good guys," Andy says.

"I guess."

He puts down his fork. "Don't worry, man. You're gonna be there with me."

"Where's that?"

"In New York. At the contest. If you don't go, who's gonna hold the bucket?"

"Wait'll I tell my dad. He's afraid I'll never amount to anything."

THREE

After school I head for the parking lot. It's almost March and colder than it's supposed to be in sunny California. The kid ahead of me is just about lost in his hoodie. I'm listening to "What's Got Me Down" (U.S. Mail Band, for the record). I don't have to look real hard for Andy's car. Stevie Wonder could find a Corolla between a Firebird and a Ford F-150.

When my cell rings, I know it's either Andy or my mom. My favorites list is a tiny principality with two citizens.

"I got detention, man," Andy says. "And I've got this thing to do for Mr. Kanenobu."

"He's letting you talk on the phone?"

"Nah, he's in the can. Man, I wish we were in Alaska. Twenty-four-hour buffets all day. Whales and bears when we get shore leave. You'll be the ship's DJ, and I'll carve mermaids out of ice with a chain saw like those guys on TV do. Oops, here comes Mr. Kanenobu. I gotta go."

I'm barely at the bus stop when Chris Teagarden pulls up in his Mustang. Four guys pile out. I shrug off my book bag. There's a kind of guy who would taunt Chris, call him chicken shit for having so much backup, and engage in semi-cordial and predictably coded trash talk, basically trying to get out of fighting altogether. I am not that guy. I wade right in.

I've got two of them backing away and whimpering when I get grabbed from behind and dropped hard. Somebody else shoves something gross in my mouth, and I gag and cough.

One of them points his camera phone at me. "This'll go right to the Net, faggot. I'll tell you how many hits you get."

Chris dabs at his nose, and grins at the blood. "Tell your fat friend he's next, Glazier. I mean it." Then they all sprint for Chris's Mustang.

That thing in my mouth turns out to be a carrot. A big dirty carrot. Two girls who are waiting for the bus ask, "Do you know him?"

I take a deep breath and get to my feet. My hand hurts and I look at it fondly. "That was the Good

Samaritan's evil twin, the one you don't hear so much about."

The short one says, "He's cute."

That's when I see the mammoth. The graffiti one Allyssa was talking about in math. It's all over the side of the bus and it's orange. Or its outline is. But I can tell what it's supposed to be—a big old *Mammuthus primigenius*. Complete with tusks. Right from the Pleistocene. What a relief that would be—something somebody can do something about. Mammoths in the street. Mammoths at the middle school. *Invasion of the Mammoths*. I'm not the only person who would abandon his medications and sorrows and suit up.

"You okay, man?"

I look at this kid Lemar from my gym class and nod.

"I saw it," he says, "if you want to tell anybody. You didn't do nothin'."

I shake my head. "It's cool. But thanks."

In an hour or so the evening really will spread out against the sky. Cocktails for the folks, but for you and me it's Chemical Imbalance covering "Convenience Store Hot-Shots."

Dad's car is in the driveway. I bet Mom wants him to sing with her group. He used to like it. Now she has to tell him to come home from the lab; sometimes he stays all night. Pretty soon there he'll be between Mr. Graham who always wears a peacock vest and Mrs. Larkin with the big boobs. He'll want nothing to do with Vega, the tenor, who always has one sleeve rolled up so everybody can see his cobra tattoo. Mr. Vega lives in a kind of Tudor McMansion a few miles from here and does the whole landed-gentry thing. Cut glass, a harpsichord, and a picture over the fireplace of a huge, elegant cow at her repose.

Inside I lean back against the door and listen to Mom start those up-and-down-the-scales warm-up exercises. Her yoga pad hangs on the coat rack in its soft, purple quiver. Her loose pants have got an elephant pattern but not just any elephant. It's Ganesh, who, Mom says, brings joy and happiness to the family and removes all obstacles.

Well, if Ganesh is going to do that kind of work around here, he'll need overalls and some power tools.

"Ryan!"

My mother lays some sheet music on the piano. We look a lot alike except that she's pretty and in great shape.

"Are you all right?" she asks.

"You should see the other guys."

"Oh, Ryan. Not again."

"It was across the street from the school. Nobody's going to call you."

Her arms go around me. "They'd better not. Go wash your face. When everybody gets here, will you be a bartender for ten minutes or so? It's just red wine and white wine, and Vega's single malt."

"Okay, I guess."

"And will you change for me?" She takes hold of my shirt. "This is almost threadbare."

I pretend to bat at her. "Keep your hands off this T-shirt. This is classic Bob Marley."

She turns to my father, who's reading some science magazine. "Look at this thing," she says. "Look at the condition it's in! My son the urchin. Separated from loving parents by cruel Fortune, he roams the cobbled streets alone."

She's trying hard, and I can feel the strain. She prefers to handle things gingerly. Which is better than coming home with a bloody nose, I have to admit. So if she wants me to serve drinks, I'll serve drinks.

I look behind the bar. Sure enough—red wine, white wine, and Mr. Vega's Scotch. I pour my dad some room-temperature club soda. No ice ever in anything for him. Something he read somewhere about how cold drinks make the heart work harder. He pampers his body like an only child. Mine is like Andy's car—just something to get around in. Sometimes I look at my dad, and he's like nobody I ever knew.

I hold the glass out.

He asks, "How was school?"

I lean across the little bar. Just a couple of guys chatting over a drink. "How do you want to play this?" I ask. "If I say, 'School is fine,' then you'll say, 'If it's so fine, why aren't you getting better grades?' And if I say, 'Same old, same old,' you'll say, 'What kind of attitude is that?'"

"Am I that predictable?"

I nod. "I knew you'd say that."

He gives a little snort and turns away.

Mom made pasta, but at the other end of the table is his dinner—bean pâté, lentils and rice, broccoli and cauliflower. When Molly was dying, Dad went vegan. That's one of the reasons he's so thin. And then there's the running. A lot of runners are lean, but he's scary lean. He's cold all the time and wears little black skullcaps so he looks like a medieval scholar—skeletal and preoccupied with higher things.

His closet is a shrine to deliberate choice, mostly clones of an original getup so he doesn't have to think about what to wear. And he's smart. Ph.D. smart. Jet Propulsion Lab smart. Fumarolic conditions on Mars smart.

Mom hands me a plate of pasta. It's wonderful. Catharsis with red sauce. It makes me want to speak Italian, own a little blue boat, and fish for a living.

Let's hear it for some real food: Leigh Perry brings "Roast Fish and Cornbread," Calypso King and the Soul Investigators show up with "Brand New Potatoes," and Pink Floyd gets there just in time for dessert—"Candy and a Currant Bun."

I move the dish with his cauliflower on it a few inches to the left. "How can you eat this stuff? Try the pasta."

"I ran into Dr. Williams today. He said your glucose is creeping toward diabetes. It's not your mother's cooking that's doing it, either. It's the crap you eat when you're not home."

I put down my fork. "Why did you talk to him? He's my doctor."

"You're a minor. And, anyway, I'm worried about you. I don't want you getting sick. Your mother's been through enough."

"Not everything is my fault, Dad."

Mom steps between us, hands in the air. "Gentlemen, stop your engines."

I tell her, "I'm doing my best here, and then he starts in on me."

He tells her, "Somebody has to do something. You stand on your head and go, *'Ooommmm,'* and he shoves those things in his ears and ruins his hearing."

"Leave her alone, and don't talk about me like I'm not here."

My mother tells me, "Go upstairs, Ryan."

"Why doesn't he go somewhere? Why is it always me?"

"Now," my father says, "now who's talking about who like he's not here."

I turn right into him, so close I can smell the weird aftershave he uses. "Fine. *You* go upstairs for a change, okay? Go to *your* room."

"Let's get this straight: I'm the grown-up; you're the kid."

Just then we all hear a car door slam, and Mom says, "Ryan, please."

"Fine." But I've got a parting shot, and I wait until I'm halfway up the stairs. I'm an anti-Cupid with a little dart of venom. "And, by the way, it's 'talking about *whom* like he's not here,' okay? Not 'who.' 'About' is a preposition."

I'm a little disappointed in my personal discipline, a little surprised that he can still get to me. He shouldn't have talked to my doctor; he's *my* doctor. But do I really care? No. So I feel exonerated and petty.

I stop by what used to be Molly's bedroom. I open the door and step in. The place is always cold. Some technician came by, checked the ducts from the heater, and shrugged.

Once this was going to be Dad's office, so there's a desk in one corner but no chair. Then it was going to be Mom's room. She'd sew or do yoga. There are two posters on the wall: the Buddha, of course, and Sitasamvara with his twelve arms and four heads. One gold, the other framed in bright blue. Originally, anyway. They're both kind of dull now. The room has just sucked the pigment out of them. Nobody and nothing really wants to be in there. It's essentially haunted.

In the back of my closet, there's a giant cardboard bucket of Goldfish. Not real ones but the snack kind. I eat a couple of handfuls while I slip in "Crisis" (Alexisonfire) and just stand in the sound. I don't think the world will end with a bang or a whimper. I think it will end with a tune.

I hit the space bar on my iMac, then bring up my two e-mails. The first one is from a girl in my class named Amy who wears hemp pants.

GLOBAL WARMING IS REAL. We are already on an irreversible slide toward destruction. South America's first hurricane ever is just the beginning. REMEMBER KATRINA? In 100 years mankind will be reduced to a few breeding couples at the North Pole. We are sitting on a TIME BOMB: drought, epidemics, and killer heat waves. DON'T just hide behind the veil of right-wing lies with your AC on HIGH. MAN is the endangered species. Have you seen the sign of the MAMMOTH? Support the KYOTO PROTOCOL NOW!

Amy's the queen of imaginary disasters. Wait'll something happens to *her* sister and the quixotic is replaced by the real. I hit Delete and go on to Andy's e-mail.

Well, well. There's a picture of me with a big carrot in my mouth. The bad camera angle makes it look nasty. Andy's message is two words: "CALL ME."

He doesn't even say hello. Just "Is this the gay vegetarian?"

"There were four of 'em, okay?"

"I'm picking you up at ten."

"Good. I'd like to knock the crap out of my dad, but that's just too predictably oedipal. I'll take it out on Chris. But why so late?"

"Because *Deal or No Deal* is on. We'll be lucky if Chris isn't already beat to a pulp by the time we get there. Everybody hates him. All he does is piss people off. If he died tomorrow, there'd be a thousand suspects."

"I know two girls who take the bus who think he's cute."

"Well, I know ten more who want to cut out his heart and eat it on a stick. I'm coming at ten. Wear black. What are you eating?"

"Goldfish crackers."

"I love those things. Bring some, okay?"

. . .

Just before 10:00 P.M., I find my iPod and go downstairs. Mom's got the Bose cranked up, so her *The Magic Flute* fights with my "Sometimes I Wish I Was a Pretty Girl."

I'm halfway down the stairs when I hear the argument:

Him: "Maybe you need to go back to work."

Her: "Why would I do that? You make a ton of money."

Him: "I make a ton of money because I'm good at what I do. What are you good at? Staying home and talking on the phone?"

I don't want to get right in the middle, so I back up a few steps, then come clomping down. My dad's sitting at the far end of the couch. They look like people in a bus station. Strangers in the night.

I tell them, "I might meet Andy and stay out for a little while."

"Back by eleven." Mom doesn't open her eyes.

I nod. "I know, but I've got an hour. Anyway, it's Friday night."

"Then be careful."

My father says, "I've told you this before. You see too much of Andy. He's older than you are."

"So?"

"Why doesn't he have friends his own age?"

"He does."

Dad shakes his head. "No, he doesn't."

"You don't know anything about Andy."

He says, "I know what I know."

"Oh, great. A tautology."

"You shouldn't be going out, anyway," my father says. "Your mother and I said no fighting, and you come home looking like you took the worst of it."

"I didn't start it. And it was after school, so—"

Mom waves me away. "Stop it," she says. "Go do whatever it is you're going to do for fifty-five minutes."

As I start for the door, I'm fiddling with my iPod, looking at the album cover. My father stands up. "And take those stupid things out of your ears."

I turn around. "I'm leaving. What's the difference?"

"Either take 'em out or stay at home."

My ravaged high-tops sink into the deep carpet. The house I live in is beautiful. There's not a vulgar inch of anything anywhere. I feel like lying down right where I am and playing dead. Instead I tug on the little wires, let them dangle almost to my knees, then turn around and show him.

"Eleven o'clock, Ryan. And not eleven oh one."

When I close the door behind me, I head west. Andy will come up the hill in his Junkmobile, and I want to head him off. I don't want my dad rushing out here to riffle through Andy's all-too-available glove compartment.

When I spot his Corolla, I wave.

"Did you bring the Goldfish?" he asks.

I shake my head and jump in. "I forgot."

He holds out a joint. "Not too much. We have to be sharp tonight, and you're kind of a lightweight."

I shake my head. "I have to be back in an hour."

"I'm telling you, man. I graduate and save up some money; then you graduate, and we're out of here."

"Sure."

I get in. Andy's got a tall can of malt liquor between his legs. When he hands it to me, some spills.

I chide him, "That was smooth. Now I'll smell like a brewery. Pull over. I'd better drive. If we get stopped, the worst they can do is put my pants in jail."

As we tool down the curving streets of Rancho Palomino and right onto Foothill Boulevard, Andy says, "Route Sixty-six." He points at the four-lane street. "We should take it all the way to the East Coast."

I hear him, but we have crossed the border into Make-Believe. This next question will bring us back. "What do you think Charlotte Silano is doing tonight?"

"Are you kidding?"

"I guess we'd know if she got better all of a sudden."

Andy shakes his head. "Cynthia Wixen's blog says she's officially in a coma."

"Do you think when you're in a coma, you can smell things? I hate the way hospitals smell."

"Beats me, man."

I glance over at him. Same sneaks with the broken laces, same cargo pants, different T-shirt. "Here's a question you can answer—what happened to the part of the plan where we both wore black?"

"Are you kidding? Black makes me look fat."

I'm still laughing when a Mustang like Chris's pulls alongside us, then hangs a right. I tell Andy, "Teagarden probably isn't going to be home. It's Friday night."

"He's home." Andy lights up and takes two or three quick little hits. "He plays poker till midnight, then goes over to Cynthia Wixen's when the game breaks up."

"How do you know that?"

"Everybody knows that."

We pass Myrtle Avenue, the north-south street that cuts through downtown and runs into the 210 freeway. Almost all the stores are owned by locals, and some of them go back to the Stone Age, probably. When Molly and I were little, Mom would take us to Lohman's Hardware, where her dad bought her first Radio Flyer. She knew the patriarch behind the cash register. She knew his kid selling somebody a hose, and his kid's kid out back sharpening lawn mowers. Mr. Lohman would give us suckers, and Molly liked to let the handle of hers stick out of her mouth and waggle around like a rat's tail. The Lohmans were happy sitting around the dinner table at night talking about fertilizer and finishing nails. And for all I know, they still are.

"I can't wait to get out of this place," says Andy. "Monrovia's a stupid name."

"It's not named for President Monroe; it's named for Bill Monroe, who owned a bunch of land around here."

"Like that makes a difference," says Andy. He drains the can of Colt 45 and tosses it out the window. "I can't believe you know this stuff."

"It's all they talked about in grade school. Don't you remember? I knew the history of Monrovia before I could trace around my hand and make a turkey."

"You know what I remember from grade school? Fifty-nine fish sticks in fifteen minutes."

"I heard about that. Then you threw up, right?"

"Not until I got my five dollars."

Off to my right I can see the freeway that carries people west toward Los Angeles or all the way to Malibu, where the sea hisses like peroxide. As Andy just said: Like that makes a difference.

"Houses and more houses," he chants. "Buy a two-bedroom for half a mil and work so hard to pay for it, all you have time to do in it is sleep and take a crap before you hit the freeway again."

Sometimes my mind is like a crow. It just takes off on its own. Under me are clotheslines, a barbed-wire fence trampled almost flat, clover, buffalo grass, roads narrowing into nothing.

Andy nudges me. "Did you hear what I just said?"

I tell him, "REM says 'Welcome to the Occupation.' If I had it, I'd play it for you."

"Sure you don't want to finish this?" he asks, and he passes me the joint in his left hand.

I shake my head. "Not while I'm driving."

And not while the mind-crow circles Saint Mary's, then settles on just the right ledge. In the ICU that day, I could see Charlotte had a little perpendicular crease in her forehead. Who wouldn't be perplexed? The crow cocks his head and looks hard at her.

I ask Andy, "Remember the day Charlotte Silano wrote YES on one eyelid and NO on the other, and all day when anybody asked her a question, she'd close one eye?"

"Sure. You or I'd try that and end up in the principal's office. But precious Charlotte Silano does it and it's cute."

"Do you think she's still the same?"

"As when she did that? No. As when you asked nine minutes ago? Yes. Now stop thinking about her and pay attention," he rasps. "We're getting close."

He's always a little hoarse because he smokes almost constantly. I might remember where Teagarden lives, anyway. I went to a birthday party there in third grade.

Predictably, Chris pushed almost everybody into the pool.

We pass a big sign—COLUMBINE HILLS. It was named that before the shooting in Colorado, but Columbine Hills always had a bad vibe. Foundations cracked, roofs leaked, and whole lawns washed away when it rained. The developer made promises and then split. Now things catch on fire, and the cops find meth labs or patios full of organic cannabis.

I ease up to Crespi Avenue. Andy whispers, "Seventeen oh two."

"Father Crespi was the guy who came with Portola in seventeen sixty-nine."

Andy turns to me. "You know what? I'll call Teagarden out here and you bore him to death. How about that?"

I point to a retaining wall that's been pretty much washed away. What's left is covered with a brand-new orange mammoth. "You seen those?" I ask.

Andy nods. "Probably Teagarden did it. He's an anarchist."

"Bullshit. Who says?"

"Cynthia Wixen."

A porch light goes on, and a guy with a beard comes out of his house with something—a tarp, maybe—under his arm. He throws that over a motorcycle with a tall sissy bar on the back, then turns and stares at the street. He's built kind of square, like a character in a video game.

I put my foot on the gas and ask Andy, "Think he made us?"

"No way he knows the Mysterymobile." Then he reaches into the backseat. "Check this out." I'm thinking weed from Colombia, because Andy is the king of the predictable surprise. But this time he comes up with a gun. Or something like a gun.

"It's just a Tippmann," Andy explains. "But it'll get the job done."

"You want me to shoot Chris with paintballs?"

"No, we're gonna trash his car."

"Oh man, I don't know."

My hands are sweaty on the steering wheel. Between here and San Diego or here and Santa Barbara or here and Palm Springs, there must be a hundred places just like Columbine Hills. A hundred kids like Teagarden. And Andy. And me. What a depressing thought.

I ask Andy, "How do you shoot this thing?"

"Try pulling the trigger."

I touch the skinny, kind of sticky barrel, then look at my fingers. "Are you sure this is a good idea?"

Andy grins. "Are you kidding? Chris loves that car of his."

"If we get caught, my mom'll come down and bail me out, but my dad will disown me. Who knows who will get my share of the kingdom."

"Don't be a pussy," Andy says. "Chris made you blow a carrot and then took a picture."

I slow down when I point the gun out the window, so we kind of ghost past Chris Teagarden's house. In the driveway is his red Mustang, an old RV with a dirt bike strapped to the back, and a scummy-looking boat on a trailer.

I pull the trigger four or five times, then mash the accelerator.

"Did you hit it?" he asks.

"I hit something. I heard 'em go *splot*." I take a deep breath, then let it out. I don't know how I feel about this: I like it and I don't like it. I'm glad I did it, and I'm ashamed of myself. "This is really going to piss him off."

"In general, yeah. But he's not going to know it was us. Now stop worrying, and let's go someplace and celebrate."

"I'm supposed to be home by eleven."

"It's Friday night. You're not a twelve-year-old girl."

"My dad'll ground me."

"And your mom will reduce your sentence to zero. C'mon, I'm hungry."

Burger Town is almost deserted.

"You want to go in?" Andy asks. "Or drive through."

"I don't care."

"Let's go in. We've got the whole place to ourselves."

I point to four muddy-looking bicycles lying on their sides in a line like dead antelope. Very safari-like. All this picture needs is four guys in khaki, some rifles, and a whiskey and soda or two for the bwanas.

"Kids," says Andy. "Who cares."

The light inside bulldozes us into the "Order Here" line. But the music is a watered-down version of "Let's Spend the Night Together." A cover of a cover of a cover. The Stones can still howl this song. The Burger Town version barely bleats.

"Hey, guys. What'll it be?"

I know the kid behind the counter from health ed. I check his name, anyway. Elton. Yeah, that's right.

"Nice hat," says Andy.

Elton nods. "It goes with the vest."

"I noticed." Andy turns to me. "Couple of burgers, or do you want to go straight to the Oreo Delight?"

I shake my head. "I'm not the one with the munchies."

"How about two burgers and we split a large fries?"

"Okay, I guess."

Elton nods and starts punching in the order. "Two burgers, large—"

"No, no," Andy says. "Four burgers. One large fries. Two Diet Cokes. Big ones."

I tell him, "I don't want a Coke, and I don't want—"

"It's diet, man. It doesn't count. You got any money?"

"This was your idea."

"I brought the gun."

I look at Elton. "Not a real gun."

Elton shrugs. "Whatever. You can't believe the stuff I hear." He takes my money, opens the register, counts out some change. "I'll bring it over. We aren't exactly busy tonight."

We walk by four kids who are dunking fries in a big pool of ketchup. I remember hanging around with Dylan Mosely and Keith Tierney. Guys I never see anymore. When Molly was sick, they'd still call and want to play soccer. Which was the last thing I wanted to do. Not that I could have, anyway. By then, I was stoned most of the time. At first I just bought dope from Andy, then we started to hang out.

That was right around the time I knew Molly wasn't going to get better, and when that knowledge or insight hit me (*Bam! Pow!*), I more or less went numb. It was such a pummeling that I never felt a thing. Which was good. And when that numbness started to melt away, I stopped Andy Rey in the hall after French and said, "Anything going on?" And he said, "Maybe."

I know that sounds easy, but high school is easy. Everybody knows everything, and nobody tells anybody outside the faith. Andy knew I wasn't a narc—I was four-teen, for one thing—and it was common knowledge that Andy was a big, friendly slob who sold weed. Just like everybody knew Chris Teagarden was (and is) a sadist and a punk, and Patty Dean puts out on the fourth date.

So I exchanged the goals I'd had—soccer player, honor student, non-virgin—for others. One other. I wanted to get lost. Not stoned out of my mind, just less aimless and sad.

Andy settles into the booth. It's a tight fit and his gut squishes up and part of it kind of lies on the table. I know if this was a horror film, his stomach would come after me and I'd have to stab it with a fork.

"I got a little high last night," Andy says, "while I was watching MTV. And you know what I was thinking?"

"If I say the name Onan, will I be somewhere in the ballpark?"

"No, no. I was thinking that one thing I can never do is dive off the stage and have my fans catch me."

"Your fans."

"People who come to see me."

"See you do what—go to high school and get detention?"

Andy shakes head. "No. Sing. Play drums. Whatever."

"You can't do those things."

Andy leans—tries to lean—across the table. "If I

could, though, I couldn't stage-dive." He pats his seriously big stomach. "I gotta lose some weight."

"I'll tell my dad you've finally got a goal."

Andy bites the end off the little sleeve that keeps soda straws clean, then he blows it at me. I bat it away. And the next one.

Molly and I used to do that when we came here after my soccer games. Almost always with some of the other guys. And another little sister or brother. Or an older one who drove us. I didn't smoke then. I was nimble and quick. Like Jack and his famous candlestick.

"Did you see Jay's hand?" Andy asks.

I'm glad to come back from the past. "Jay Croft? Yeah. He got mad at Nona and took it out on a locker."

"Nona." Andy sounds disgusted. "Who names their kid Nona?"

"She's from the Philippines."

"She's in America now, okay? Get an American name. I'm telling you, man. We're better off without chicks." He starts ticking off names: "Yoko and the Beatles, Courtney and Nirvana, some groupie and Axl Rose."

"Axl Rose ruined Guns N' Roses all by himself."

Just then Elton brings our food on two little red trays.

"Here's a tip," says Andy. "Number seven in the first race at Upside Downs."

"Gee, I've never heard that one before."

"Thanks, Elton."

"See you, Ryan."

Andy raises his Diet Coke. "Special Ops rules. We struck under cover of darkness, accomplished our mission, and returned unscathed."

"I can't wait for my medal from a grateful nation."

Three tables away, a cell phone rings. One of the kids digs for it and immediately starts lying, "Sure I'm at Blake's. Yeah. His mom said we could stay up till eleven. Okay. Fine. Whatever." He hangs up and tosses the phone toward the ketchup.

"When did you start lying?" I ask.

Andy was eavesdropping, too. "To my folks? I'd be like three and my mom would say, 'Where are you going, honey?' And I'd say, 'To the moon.'"

"My dad talked to my doctor today without even telling me."

"Isn't that against the law?"

"I'm a minor."

Andy eats five fries at a time. For a second it looks like he's got nine fingers. "What did he talk to your doctor about?" he asks.

"I guess I'm not as healthy as I used to be."

"Didn't you already know that?"

"From talking to Dr. Williams?" I shake my head. "I took the physical, but I didn't go back."

He points. "You definitely shouldn't finish that burger."

I push the whole tray across the table.

Andy says, "My dad told me when I graduate, I have to help with the rent. I already pay Mom to do my laundry."

"Your dad's hard-core."

"I'm splitting. You know that. But until I do, I have to get some kind of job."

"What about sales and customer satisfaction?"

Andy shakes his head, but his dirty blond hair doesn't move. "I don't know. Maybe. As much as I smoke, I'm working with a narrow profit margin now." He points to the last of the fries. "You gonna eat those?"

"Help yourself."

Andy frowns. "I was losin' my buzz, anyway, but thinking about going to work, man . . ." He pokes at the ice with his straw. He sails the lid of his drink at me. "Let's get out of here."

I start to stand up. Andy goes back to Elton at the counter, gets a couple of coffees with lids on them, then comes toward me.

"What's that for?" I ask. "I don't want that."

"Not for you, man. It's for Kyle. I'm gonna go by his place after I drop you. He's been playing some old Atari game for like seven hours straight."

When we pass that table of BMXers, they start

mooing and cracking up. Andy leans in so far, they put up their hands like they're afraid he might let one of them have it. Then he says, "In Japan, fuckers, I am a sumo god."

That night I have two dreams, one right after the other. In the first one, Molly is eight and I'm ten. I'm teaching her to play Frisbee. At first she's not very good, but pretty soon—you know how dreams are—she's older and a lot better. She wants me to throw harder and farther, so I do, and she runs after it in her blue shorts and her silver shoes. Except I don't know my own strength, and I throw it so far and she runs so fast that I can barely see her. I yell that I'm sorry and ask her to come back, but she just stays out there, and pretty soon there's this kind of mist and she disappears.

Charlotte's in the next one. It's not a sexy dream, but in it I'm totally aware of the hair on the back of her neck. Two curved tortoiseshell combs keep everything else in place. We're separating wheat from chaff, throwing big handfuls of it up in the air, and letting it settle. The chaff blows away. The good stuff settles around our feet, which are naked. I mean bare.

FOUR

When Molly was in the hospital the first time, a ton of people came: her friends from school with pictures they'd colored for her, those kids' parents, the guys who work with Dad at JPL, and everybody Mom ever sang with.

When she had to go back a month later, though, not so many. And nobody stayed very long. Some dad in a suit would look at his watch or mumble into his cell phone, and I just wanted to strangle him.

At the end there was only me and my mom. And, thanks to Andy, I was barely there. There's that memory— how it was at the end. And how I was.

It takes about a week for Charlotte to get out of the ICU and into a regular room of her own, but when that happens, I feel like I need to see her again. I figure if Brad and Chloe and those guys are in attendance, I just won't go in. I'll look for their cars in the parking lot—the VW convertible with the I YAM KUTE license plate or the Nissan Frontier King Cab with twenty-inch chrome wheels and a hood scoop (and you haven't lived until you've heard Brad recite those specs for about the twentieth time).

Andy's in detention, so I'm at the bus stop. I'm thinking in negatives: the lawn is unwet, the sky is uncloudy, the bus is unfast. When the 211 finally pulls up and there's another orange mammoth spray-painted on the side, this girl I'm more or less waiting with, one Gretchen Jamison, just stares.

"Are you getting on?" I ask.

"Are you kidding, Ryan?" She points to the graffiti. "Don't you know what that means? This bus could blow up."

"Probably not."

"It's a sign."

"What of?"

She holds her books up against her Hello Kitty T-shirt. "I don't know, but it is."

"It'll be okay, Gretchen. C'mon. We'll sit together."

And she takes a step back. "So we can blow up at the same time? No thanks."

The driver leans toward the door. "What's the problem?"

I tell him, "Don't ask me. I've got a bus pass."

As I take the first step up, she says, "You'll be sorry."

The word apocalypse *comes from the Greek, and it means "to lift the veil." I was maybe ten the first time I heard the word, so I looked it up. I learned that in the Bible, anyway, there were four horsemen—War, Famine, Pestilence, and Death. When I told Molly, she immediately started to worry about their horses. Did Famine carry a big bag of oats for his horse? Who took care of them at night? Was there a stable boy of the Apocalypse to give the horses baths and long drinks of water? I told her I was pretty sure the horses were all right, opened some corn chips, played her "Nights in White Satin," and put her to bed with a light on.*

The hospital is air-conditioned, but I'm sweating. I know Charlotte's room number but I ask, anyway. I'm stalling for time. I could just go back to the bus stop. But I don't.

A couple of interns go by pushing a bald lady in a wheelchair. She's got on those bunny slippers with the big ears and a pink robe. Mom brought Molly's pajamas (the ones with the sleepy sheep), and it just made things worse. For me, anyway. I mean she was dressed like she used to be, but no way was she anything like she used to be.

The elevator is testing me. It doesn't ascend; it oozes

up its gloomy shaft. I've got plenty of time to cut and run. I start thinking about an old blues song called "St. James Infirmary." Somebody's on a long, white table, and she's still and cold and bare.

Ping! The paneled elevator is empty except for a long, white feather in one corner. That gives me something to think about: How did it get there? Did someone bring a bird into the hospital? Or is it something that fell out of some weird bouquet delivered by a bored driver?

That gets me to the fifth floor. When the door opens, somebody is sobbing among five or six zoned-out strangers. An older woman is patting the weeper so mechanically she might have been wound up. Everybody else is staring at the TV. I particularly hated television when Molly was here. I'd go outside and smoke another joint while my mom pretended to watch *Jeopardy*.

I wait at the desk until the nurse closes the chart she's working on. Her name tag says MONICA. Finally I say, "Excuse me. Is it okay if I go see Charlotte Silano?"

She still doesn't look up. "Well, sure. Just keep it brief."

"Don't worry about that."

Monica takes a bite of a doughnut dusted with a powder so white it looks festive.

I make my way down the hall, watching the numbers climb: 525, 527, 529. I hated going from the elevator to

Molly's room. Because once I got there, I knew what I was going to find. She was always glad to see me, though, no matter how addled I was. One of the last things she said was, "Remember when we pretended to be squirrels, Ryan?" I just had to turn around, go to the window, and stand there. It was night, and I thought I could feel the moon pulling at me.

Then I'm almost to 531. Charlotte's room. I lean until my forehead's against the wall. I take a deep breath and go inside, but barely.

I think about some lyrics I ought to know but don't. Something about fresh towels and a tall, cool drink. The blinds on the far side of the room make a shadow ladder on the opposite wall, a ladder only a spider could climb.

I promised myself I wouldn't get high this time. Why did I do that?

I get closer, anyway. It's her all right, even with no makeup and her hair in braids. More freckles than I remember. There's the IV leading into her arm and—on the other side of the bed—a see-through bag.

The mind-crow watches a rabbit stop, then bolt. A nearby pond looks hot on the surface and silvery. I make the rabbit come back, calling with a whistle nothing else can hear.

There are a couple of chairs with metal arms, so I back into the one not occupied by a teddy bear with a bow tie. There's a vase of tired-looking flowers on an aluminum chest of drawers, probably for keeping sheets and those gowns that open in the back. Lots of photographs taped to the walls: Charlotte and Jill on skis, Charlotte at Halloween with painted-on cat whiskers, Charlotte arm in arm with her parents in front of the Eiffel Tower, Charlotte and Derek all dressed up. Everybody in every shot looks happy.

I pick up that giant card, the one with the sad horse. Derek didn't even bother to write his name. He's so good-looking he's useless.

It's really weird to see Charlotte like this. She was always running around, always on the go. She looks alive—there's color in her cheeks and all that—but it freaks me out that she doesn't move. Molly used to at least sit up.

I watch the readout on her monitor—respiration, oxygen levels, pulse: *throb, throb, throb.* My stomach growls and I squirm in the chair a little. She's totally quiet.

Finally I say, "My name's Ryan Glazier. I'm two years behind you in school, so you don't know me. But I just came by because I wanted to say I'm sorry you're here. Hospitals suck. Believe me, I know."

I stand up and watch her breathe. Her mouth is open a little, like somebody who is asleep. But not all gross or droolly like Andy or most people.

I sit down again. Neither one—up or down—seems right. "Your nurse's name is Monica. Did you know there's a saint named Monica? My sister, Molly, liked to read about saints. We aren't Catholic or anything like that, but Molly loved Wilgefortis. She grew a beard so she didn't have to get married."

No sign she heard a word. Water off a duck's back. Totally Teflon. I could say anything.

On my feet again, I take a little tour of the room. There's an AC/heater right below the sealed window: OFF, LOW HEAT, HIGH HEAT, LOW COOL, HIGH COOL. Charlotte used to be HIGH COOL, now she's LOW HEAT. One notch away from OFF.

Back to that chair. "You really ought to try and wake up, okay? This is hard on your folks. I know that one, too. And if you're like me and you don't get along with your folks, well, then do it for your horse."

I can hear myself admonish her, and I just feel stupid. It's like talking to the wall. I wish I had Bow Wow Wow's version of "Fools Rush In" on my iPod. I'd play it about twelve times until I got the message. What am I doing here?

"Knock, knock." Monica walks right up to me. "You want to step outside, honey. Girl stuff."

Monica just radiates health. She's capable and strong. Her uniform is spotless, and a pulse throbs in her neck. I want to kiss her. Not a sexy kiss, just on the cheek, just enough to have her put her arms around me for, like, two seconds.

I'm headed for the door when she says, "Charlotte's a lucky gal. No insurance problems, and her dad's on staff. That's why she's not in some coma warehouse. So we're glad to have her, and she's glad to be here." The nurse pats Charlotte's leg. "Aren't you, sweetie?" She smiles at me. "The patient next door could use a visitor, I bet."

"Nah, that's okay. I'll just . . ."

"It'll only take a minute."

A shrug. The Shrug. That and the word *whatever* get most kids I know through adolescence.

I peek into room 533 and there's this kid. Maybe ten years old: hospital gown, baseball cap, IV. When I walk in, he waves. I like that. There wasn't a whole lot of waving next door. His TV is on; there's a Rally Monkey peering out of a tangle of wires that lead from his bed. There are books and magazines: signs of life.

"The nurse said you could use a visitor," I say.

"Cool. Who are you really here for?"

"Charlotte Silano."

"Oh, yeah. Coma Girl. Is she your girlfriend?"

"No way."

"Because you've already got one?"

"No. Just because she's not. Have you seen her?"

"Sure."

"And you think she could ever be my girlfriend?"

"I don't know. You could rock. You could be rich. There's all kinds of reasons she could like you."

"Well, she doesn't, okay?"

"Then why are you here? Isn't she a senior?"

"You know a lot for a kid who doesn't get out of bed."

He scoots around and lets his legs dangle over the edge of the bed. Even his feet look bony. "What's your name?"

"Ryan."

"Mine's Thad." He picks up the remote and mutes the TV, where some jocks are snarling at each other. "Do you ever pretend? This lady comes in and says I should pretend to be well, and if I do it right, pretty soon I will be. Why don't you pretend Charlotte's your girlfriend, then she will be?"

"Aren't you a little young to be thinking about romance all the time? I just came by to say hi to Charlotte."

"So it's like a good deed."

"It's no big deal."

He turns his Dodgers cap so the bill is sideways, takes a Payday candy bar off the little table right by the bed, and holds it out.

I shake my head. "No thanks. My dad's got a plate of steamed chard waiting for me."

"Sounds worse than the green Jell-O in this place."

Thad tosses the Dodgers cap off and picks up one of those Samuel L. Jackson Kangol jobs: like a driving cap or an old-fashioned golf hat. He puts it on backward and actually looks pretty cool. Under the circumstances, anyway.

He asks, "Want to hear something really mysterious? I can go to the other side. To Deadville."

Now that I think of it, he looks a little feverish. "Are you okay, man? What are these doctors giving you?"

"I go over there when I'm asleep."

"Isn't that called dreaming?"

"Nah," he says, "it's different."

Just then Charlotte's nurse leans into the room. "You can go back in now." She looks at Thad. "Need anything, honey?"

"The April *Playboy*?" He waits for the laugh, waits for her to go on back down the hall. "They crack up at almost anything," he says. "According to them, I could be a stand-up comic. If I could stand up."

I'm halfway to the door when Thad motions me back. "What?" I ask.

"Just come here." He waits until I'm standing by the bed. Then he gets hold of my wrist, pulls me down, and hisses, "I see your friend in Deadville."

"Charlotte?"

He nods.

I humor him. "But she's not dead."

"Well, yeah. But she could be. There's like this waiting room, and she goes there."

I say, "I hope the magazines are better than the ones in this place." But now I want him to shut up. I wonder just how sharp a rebuke I need.

He says, "You know those stories about people after car wrecks or during operations how they look down and see their bodies and stuff and there's this tunnel of light and they've got to choose—"

"Listen, I know a little about drugs. You get behind some of that stuff, you think you see all kinds of weird things." I tug on his hat like you can do with kids. "Charlotte's going to be fine. She's got everything to live for."

Next door she looks the same, but the nurse did something. Not just a new bottle of chocolaty-looking stuff hanging over her head, either. Her nightgown's different. Not from here. From home, I bet.

I walk up to her. Did the nurse have time to wash her hair? Something smells like coconut.

"Listen," I say to her. Toward her, actually. I'm still having trouble looking her right in the eyes. Which are kind of open, by the way. "Now that I'm here, I might as well tell you something. The last time I saw you at school, I thought this crummy thing. You were twitching your butt around the cafeteria and just generally showcasing your genetic advantages, and I thought, 'Why didn't you get a brain tumor instead of my sister?'" I take a deep breath. "I didn't say it out loud and I didn't tell anybody, not even Andy. But I'm sorry. I didn't really mean it. It was just . . . I don't know. One of those crappy things people think sometimes." I take a step back and use what's left of my sense of humor. "Don't get up. I'll let myself out."

I'm barely through the door when I run into Betty Bennett. Or actually she almost runs into me because she's checking numbers left and right. She must have come straight from volleyball practice because she's in shorts and sneaks and a tank top and she's still wearing knee pads, but loose and down around her ankles. She's tall and damp. She's so totally alive. So unmarred.

"What are you doing here?" I ask.

She holds out one of those square envelopes. "Everybody on the team finally got it together and signed a card. I'm in tenth grade, so I'm the delivery boy. Girl, I mean." She turns the card in her hands. "But it's okay. I kind of wanted to see her, anyway. What about you?"

"What about me?"

"What are you doing here?"

"Oh, yeah. Well, I was just in the neighborhood . . ."

She grins and taps her nose. "Try again, Pinocchio."

"Actually my mom wanted me to drop off some little plant." I point behind me. "It's in there." Along with the other nine thousand balloons and stuffed bears. It's just a little lie, anyway.

Betty tugs at her shorts the way jocks do: for comfort, not from modesty.

"Well," she says finally. "Here we are."

"Yeah, well." I point. "I guess I'll just . . ."

"Are you leaving? Wait a minute. Let me just duck in here. Then I'll ride down with you."

I nod and lean against the wall. Girls in comas, kids who dream about someplace called Deadville, and that hospital smell. I can't wait to get outside.

When Betty comes out of Charlotte's room, she honest-to-God looks pale.

"Man," she says. "That was harder than I thought it was going to be."

I take her arm and lead her down the hall. "Tell me about it."

"I knew she wouldn't be sitting up in bed or anything, but . . . I don't know. She used to be everywhere on the court. I've seen her asleep, and she wasn't as still as she is now."

I punch the elevator button with my left hand. My right one is still holding Betty's wrist. But that's over when the door opens. Betty leans against the wall, and the minute we're on our way down to the lobby, she blurts, "I didn't just come because of that card. I came to tell her I was sorry that I called her a bitch."

"Are you serious? I apologized, too."

"For what?"

"Something I thought, but it was crummy."

Right then the door opens on the second floor. An orderly gets on. He's pushing an old guy in a wheelchair who has on flannel pajamas with a cowboy print. Gunslingers on one arm and Indians on the other. There's a rodeo on his chest.

Betty can't stand still. She stretches toward the ceiling, does a couple of squats, puts both hands on her hips, and rocks from side to side. The guy in the wheelchair stares at her.

When we are finally outside, Betty stops and leans against the nearest wall. She looks dazed, and I realize I barely know her.

"The last thing I said to her before she got hurt was, 'You're such a bitch.' Nice, huh? It was only a stupid practice, anyway."

Then she shudders, except it's not that cold at all. She says, "Didn't you just about freak out in there?"

"Absolutely."

She asks, "Do you want to get coffee or something? I feel so weird."

"I, uh. No. I mean, I have to get, you know, home."
The absolutely naked need to get high embarrasses me
and makes me tongue-tied.

"Want a ride?" She points toward the parking lot.

"I gotta go, sorry." And I trot away toward the
deserted bus stop.

Once I'm in the little shelter with its ads for insurance
and cell phones, I dig in my backpack, come up with a
joint Andy gave me, light it with my favorite yellow Bic,
and take the biggest drag I can. I'm leaning against the
scratched-up Plexiglas when Betty appears. I try and hide
the smoke.

"You're not going home," she says. "You're getting high."

"I thought you were going for coffee."

"I don't want to be by myself, okay? I'm upset."

"Well, who isn't."

"So every time you're upset, you get stoned?"

Now I inhale flagrantly, belligerently. "That's exactly
what I do."

Betty shakes her head like I've seen my mother do
when she's totally fed up. Then she stalks away. I expect
to see her disappear between SUVs, but instead she stops,
turns around, and bears down on me. For a second I think
she's going to slug me, but she only yells, "You used to be
a nice kid. Now look at you."

Then she walks away. That's when the horizon kind of tilts, and I look down at the joint in my hand, then sink until I'm sitting on the ground. I dig out my cell phone, which feels like a playing card. The lighted buttons pulse like quasars.

I'm glad when Andy answers, but I yell at him, anyway. "What was in that joint you gave me?"

"It's just a little black mo, maybe laced with some hash. It's killer, isn't it?"

"Why didn't you tell me? I feel really weird."

"You sound really weird, man. Where are you?"

"Out in front of Saint Mary's. I can't go home like this. I'm all lit up."

"How much did you smoke?"

"Just a couple of hits, but—"

"Relax, man. It'll wear off in an hour. What are you doing at the hospital?"

"I came to see Charlotte."

"How was that?" he asks. "Did you check out her boobs?"

"I gotta go. I think I see the bus. Or maybe it's one of those mammoths. Either way, I'm getting on."

The ride is bizarre. There's a lady in a green dress with big blue pockets and a down vest that leaks feathers every time she moves. And she moves a lot, squirming deeper into the seat like she's guarding something hatchable. A

Hispanic guy gets on with a white cloth tied around his biceps; it's either a sign of something—a club, an organization, a cabal—or it's a tourniquet. He sits there grimacing and flexing his fist rhythmically for at least ten blocks. I start to get paranoid.

When I see the neon sign for Burger Town, I stumble toward the front of the bus like somebody through a gauntlet. I stand outside a minute and brush at my shirt and jeans. I feel dowdy and common.

Inside, the light makes me feel like an ant under some sadistic kid's magnifying glass. When I get to the counter, Elton says, "Where's your partner, or are you gonna order a quarter pound of sizzling, artery-clogging fat just for you?"

"I'll just take a coffee."

Elton takes a good look at me. "Are you loaded?"

"Just a little. I'm okay."

"You ought to see your eyes."

"Oh, great."

"Sit down, okay? I'll get you a salad or something. Coffee white or black?"

"Little cream. Thanks, man."

I find an empty booth and sit down. There's a newspaper, and I figure I'll pretend to read that and look normal. But it's only one of those cheesy pseudo-papers with this headline: MAN BRINGS FOX-WIFE TO CLASS REUNION. Does it mean a foxy wife, somebody beautiful and the envy of the other husbands, or did he go deep into some forest and talk to a crone and now his wife sniffs the wind and sleeps with her lavish tail across her long face?

When Elton brings the food, I hand him the paper and fumble for some cash. Which he waves away.

"Somebody ordered it, then didn't want it. It was just going to go to waste, anyway. You gonna be okay?"

"Yeah, as long as these croutons don't reprimand me."

He grins. "You're not driving, are you?"

I shake my head. "Bus."

"Okay. Take your time."

I eat a little of the salad, take a sip of coffee, watch customers come and go. I'm starting to think I'll be okay. That I can hold up my end of the dinner-table conversation. That my dad won't look at me and start in.

A girl I know well enough to say hi to gets in line and stares up at the menu. She's got jaw-length, blunt-cut hair that somebody has turned copper. When she looks my way, I wave, but she pretends she doesn't see.

I want to tell her this story about the time Molly and my folks and I were at this lake dotted with Canada geese. Everything was fine until Molly found out from a girl at the concession stand that the wings of the geese were clipped so they couldn't fly. "It's good for business," she said. Which made Molly cry. Made her cry really loud. Propelling my dad off his chaise like someone shot out of a cannon. "They're prisoners," Molly wailed. The sno-cone girl just stood there stammering, "I didn't do anything. I didn't."

If I could take a little nap, I'd wake up and be fine. I put my head down on the table and close my eyes for just a minute.

The next thing I know, somebody is shaking me. Hard. He's got my T-shirt in one hand, and he's making me sit up.

"This is a family restaurant," he hisses. "Not a flophouse. Go sleep under a bridge or something."

I try and get away from him and stand on my own two feet. "Take it easy."

Elton intervenes. He actually gets between us. "C'mon, Mr. Dils," Elton says. "Ryan's okay. I know him. He's just tired. He works at night, don't you, Ryan?"

I straighten my T-shirt. "Yeah. I'm tired. I work at night."

"You two come with me. I mean it."

We follow Elton's manager—He's got to be a manager. Who else would care that much?—out a side door. On the way, Elton looks over at me and rolls his eyes.

When Mr. Dils stops, we stop. Then he turns around and starts the lecture.

"Don't come in here anymore in that condition," he says.

I say, "What condition is that? Tired? If nobody can come in here when they're tired, you are gonna go broke real fast."

"I know a stoner when I see one, okay? I started out here at night. So don't tell me you're tired."

Elton says, "Look, this is just a misunderstanding, okay? Nobody got hurt; nobody ran out screaming. Let it go."

Mr. Dils straightens his clip-on tie. "Our volume is down ten percent from last month and the weather's better. That's not supposed to happen. If some loadie in a corner booth makes just one family go someplace else to eat, that's one family too many." He points at me first. "You get out of here, and, Elton, you go back to work."

Elton takes off his flashy vest and paper hat and hands them over. "I don't think so."

Mr. Dils just stares at them. "You're quitting?"

"Looks like it." He tugs at me. "C'mon, Ryan. I'll give you a ride."

I follow him around a couple of brightly colored trash cans. Adrenaline has semi-restored my sense of equilibrium. "Sorry, man."

"Ah, I was fed up with Dils, anyway. He can be a real

pain." He points to an older Caddy: not white exactly, not anymore, anyway. But not cream-colored or beige. Spilt milk, maybe. The color of spilt milk.

"It's open."

The seats are like Wonder bread. Not that blinding hue but that soft. I let myself go as we ease out of the parking lot.

I lean back and take a deep breath. "I just nodded out in Burger Town. How low-rent is that?"

"What was the occasion, anyway?"

"Andy gave me a joint; I thought it was just regular, you know, weed, but it wasn't."

He nods. "But he knew."

"It was supposed to be a surprise."

"You're surprised you took a snooze in your salad, aren't you?"

"Not that kind."

I watch him glide out onto Colorado Boulevard. He's got a cool haircut and one of those little soul patches right under his lower lip. His shirt looks a lot better without that stupid vest: short sleeves, very blue, pressed.

I ask him, "Where'd you get your shirt?" Every time I say something that makes sense, I feel a little better. If I have to recover by increments, so be it.

"Aardvark's. I shop there a lot. Leigh and I, like, haunt that place."

"Leigh Ann, right?"

He grins. "She's fun."

I sit up a little straighter. The lights from other cars aren't so smeared and blanched. "Didn't you used to go with Betty Bennett?"

"For a while, yeah."

"What's she like?"

"Prim."

I nod. "We were at Saint Mary's together, and then when we said good-bye and I thought she was gone, I lit up. But she came back and chewed me out good. Which I maybe deserved since I was all but sprawled on the ground like a wino."

"What was going on at the hospital? Are you okay?"

"I kind of dropped in on Charlotte Silano."

"Oh, yeah. I heard about that. Somebody said she was paralyzed."

"No. She's in a coma, though."

"Her dad's a doctor," Elton says. "Can't he do anything?"

"Not yet, anyway."

Some of the streetlamps in Old Town are meant to look old, so they're green and faceted. I like the ones we're driving under, tall and gracefully arched like the necks of swans. Why doesn't one just lean down, take me in its big beak, and carry me away?

I watch Elton check out traffic in his rearview mirror. He says, "I'm gonna buy a Red Bull. Want one?"

I wave him away. "No more stimulants or depressants of any kind for me."

He wheels into a 7-Eleven, ratchets the gearshift into P, leaves the motor running. "Play the radio if you want." He points to a few skateboarders leaning on the cinder-block building. Behind them is a spray-painted outline of the mammoth. "Don't buy any weed from those guys. It's real skunky."

Elton has one of those green deodorant mini-trees hanging from his rearview mirror. I give it a little flick with one finger and watch it revolve. The hood of the car is long and cross-hatched with light, so it looks plaid. I remember one of the first times I smoked with Andy. I liked the innocent chimeras—the super-crisp edges of things, the way a bonfire up at the Flats was better than TV. Those things called attention to themselves and distracted me.

Just then those skate zombies from school come toward me. They're all nicked and broken, cut and scabbed, bruised and mangled and warped. They fall down about two hundred times a day, then get right up. Charlotte falls once. The one with a splint on his finger taps on the window, and I lower the glass an inch or two.

He says, "Ryan, I saw your dad on television talking about Mars."

"Yeah?"

"I know it's a long way away, the human part, but tell him we'd go." He glances at his pals. "We'd clean up and train and everything. We'd totally go. Tell him, okay?"

"Sure."

Elton comes through the door of the 7-Eleven pulling the tab on his energy drink.

"Hey, Waco."

"What's up, El? Just talking to the spaceman here. Catch you later."

Elton shakes his head. "That guy is always baked."

"While I only pass out in Burger Town."

Just then his cell rings, and I half listen to half a conversation. I like the tempo of it best: a horse laugh or two punctuated with murmurs I'm almost supposed to hear.

He hangs up just as I point to my driveway. As we roll to a stop, I tell him, "Thanks for the ride, man. I really didn't mean for you to quit your job. And I'm totally sorry I dozed off like that."

Elton holds his fist out. "Don't worry about it. I was just lookin' for an excuse to move up in the food service industry, anyway."

I make my way around the front of the car, stop right beside him, and ask, "How do I look?"

"Better. Are your folks home?"

"Mom is for sure."

"Stay in the shadows."

I watch him pull away, then walk past the lawn jockey at the start of the driveway with his politically correct beige face. He's about the size of a famous dwarf named Joseph Boruwlaski that Dad told Molly and me about. The part she liked best is a made-up part—how his wife would get mad at Joseph, put him up on a shelf, and walk out of the room. And Dad would do that to Molly, swoop down and plop her on the mantle, and then pretend to leave, except what he'd actually do is make a big U turn, grab her off her perch, and bury his face in her neck until Mom made them stop before Molly threw up.

Toward the back of the lawn are some Adirondack chairs, and I make my way there. If I've got a plan (and I don't), it's to sit outside where it's cool and gather my wits. Through the French doors, Mom stands by the stove and Dad sits at the kitchen table solving one Sudoku puzzle after another. Every now and then, she says something and then he does. They seem a lot happier without me.

Well, well. If it isn't Self-Pity with her little lariat. Time to go in and face the music. In this case, the Mozart.

When I close the front door behind me, Dad looks up from his puzzles. "You're supposed to call if you're going to be late," he says.

"I know, I forgot. I'm sorry."

"No, you're not. That's just something you say. Come here, Ryan. What's wrong with your eyes? Are you on drugs?"

I put my book bag down, drop it on purpose, lean to get it, tilt it so stuff falls out. Anything to stall for time. I cross the kitchen. It feels a lot hotter than it is. When my mom opens the oven, all I can think about is poor Hansel.

"No, I'm not on drugs. I've been crying, okay?"

That makes my mother turn around. She's got crocodile oven mitts on both hands, and their long snouts open and close slowly. "Honey," she says, "what in the world about?"

"I went to the hospital see Charlotte Silano. That was bad enough, but it reminded me of . . . Well, you know what it reminded me of."

My dad looks at me like I'm some kind of third-rate troubadour who doesn't deserve even a bowl of soup, his tale is so preposterous.

Mom hands me a paper towel. "Blow your nose." She lays out three plates. "Oh, the girl who fell off her horse. I heard about it in yoga. How's she doing?"

"Not so good. She's in a coma."

"That poor family. I didn't know you two were friends."

"We're not really. I don't know why I went by. I just

did." I pick up a napkin and dab at my eyes. "And it was awful."

"I know her mother from PTA. Charlotte's a couple of years ahead of you, right?"

"Uh-huh."

My mother says, "She was a beautiful girl." She hands my father silverware and napkins, and I watch him dole them out. "Don't you know her dad? Isn't he a doctor?"

My father nods. "He thought he was a runner. I buried him after three miles."

"Right after yoga," Mom says, "a few of us stayed and did visualization. We saw her on her feet and at school."

My father leans back in his chair. "A lot of good that will do." He looks at me again. I know he knows, and I know he's going to let it go. He's not smirking at me, either. He's the kind of rational humanist who believes in a vast commonality, even though he's super-smart and not common at all. But we were walking somewhere together about four years ago, and he said he liked to believe that every time we breathed, we inhaled a molecule of Shakespeare's breath. Which I thought then and now, too, is a very cool idea. Except right at this moment, it looks like he believes I've been giving mouth-to-mouth to someone like Judas.

Mom brings a casserole to the table, and Dad shifts his adzuki beans away from it. "My yoga teacher says there's this threshold, and that's where people like Charlotte choose whether or not to go on."

Dad shakes his head and reaches for his super-oxygenated-direct-from-Valhalla-glacier water. "Your yoga teacher sells Amway products on the side."

"I'm just telling you what he said."

I feel like a thief in one of those caper movies, a thief who's had the presence of mind to bring an enormous steak with him to distract the Dobermans who would otherwise tear him limb from limb. The story of Charlotte is that steak.

When the phone in the hall rings, Mom says, "Tell whoever it is we're eating."

When I answer, a girl's voice says, "Ryan? I just wanted to make sure you got home all right."

"Betty?"

"Yeah. So you're okay? You sound okay."

"For somebody who used to be a nice guy."

"Sorry about that. Am I interrupting something?"

"I was just lying to my parents."

"Well, I called to apologize. I came on a little strong at the hospital. At the bus stop, actually. It's not like you were blowing smoke on Charlotte. What you do is none of my business. I hadn't had the best day in the world, anyway. I shouldn't have taken that out on you."

"Your day sounds as bad as mine. Charlotte freaked

me out, I got loaded, you yelled at me, and I got Elton fired from his job."

"How'd you get Elton fired?"

"I did something stupid at Burger Town, he tried to help me out, his manager got kind of unreasonable, so Elton quit."

"Elton likes to quit," she tells me. "We went out for a while, and he must have had five jobs."

"Seriously?"

"Seriously we went out, or seriously he had five jobs?"

I shift the phone to my other ear. "He just seems like such an easygoing guy."

"To go out with me?"

"To get fired all the time."

"No, no. He doesn't get fired. He quits. I've seen him in about seven of those funny-looking vests."

I sit down on the couch. Under the glass on the coffee table, there are dozens of seashells. We used to go places to snorkel, and Molly would bring home bags of souvenirs.

"For the record? I know you guys went out. He told me."

"Did he say anything else?"

"He said you were prim."

"Who wouldn't be? He smelled like French fries."

My mom comes to the archway and stands there with that "What's going on?" look on her face.

"Ryan?" Betty says.

"Yeah. Sorry. I think my folks want me to finish eating."

"I'll let you go, then. I just wanted to say I'm sorry, okay?"

"Sure. Thanks. I'll see you tomorrow."

On my way back to the kitchen, I'm really tired. I kind of feel like I've had the flu but now I'm better and need to sleep for fourteen hours.

When I get to the table, my mother asks, "Who was that?"

"A girl from school."

"Is she nice?"

"Yes."

"Is she pretty?"

"Except for the fangs and the limp. I know where you're going with this, Mom, so don't. Look, I think—"

"Don't anybody go anywhere for a minute," my father says. He uses his chopsticks to move some baked tofu around on his plate. "On the way home from the lab today, I joined a gym." He looks at me. "We did. They had this two-for-one deal, so I signed us up."

That gets my attention. "A gym."

"What'd I just say? Yes, a gym. Dr. Williams thinks it'd be good for both of us."

The absurdity of this restores me to my ususal difficult self. "Did you even think about asking me first?"

Dad puts down one chopstick. Probably so he won't plunge it into my heart. "You'd say no."

I tell him, "I might not. I'd just like to be asked for once: 'Ryan, do you want to join a gym? We could work out together. I'd gain a little weight, and you'd lose a little.' 'Yeah, maybe. Let me think about it.' Why don't I ever hear that instead of 'I signed you up and you're going'?"

Dad takes a big breath and says, "Have your mother buy you some clothes. I don't want you looking like a bum."

Mom leans forward. "'Have your mother buy you some clothes'? I'm with Ryan on this one. How about 'Melanie, would you mind getting Ryan some clothes to work out in, please?'"

He points the other chopstick at her. "Don't you start, too."

She asks, "Why are you so difficult, Robert? Talking to you is like—"

My father snaps, "I'm tired, all right? I work hard and

I'm tired, and getting anybody to cooperate around here is like pulling teeth."

"Then don't work so hard. You didn't used to work so hard."

"And do what?" my father asks. "Sit around here and listen to you talk to Vega?"

My mother sighs. "He's a singer. I talk to my singers all the time."

All that's left of my buzz is a headache. "I'm going to pass on this rerun, okay?"

FIVE

Next morning I'm sitting out in front of the school, revisiting the series of events both large and small that got me to this point. An inventory that gives me a slight case of vertigo. That was a bad scene yesterday outside the hospital and then at Burger Town. I never want to do that again.

I'm also watching some ninth-grader and his girlfriend on the lawn. They're playing tag or something like tag. She's in a thrift-store miniskirt, boots, and a shimmery top. He's in an orange hoodie, but he doesn't look like an ad for vitamin C.

"Give up, rookie," she says, teasing him. "You're never gonna get me."

But he is. She wants him to. She's going to let him.

Andy plops down next to me. "Hey, man. Interested in a little jive stick?"

I poke his big, soft shoulder. "As Moby-Dick said, 'Thanks for the harpoon.'"

"So when I get this next shipment with the elephant tranquilizer and the rocket fuel, you don't want any, right?"

I nod and say, "That stuff gave me bad dreams."

"No complaints from my other customers."

"Yeah? Well, they hadn't been in Deadville's waiting room reading old *National Geographics*."

Just then Jill Warner stops, rubs at her eyes, and says to Andy, "Anything going on?"

I haven't seen her since that time in the ICU when everybody was there. The day Charlotte fell. I take in Jill's flip-flops and the grungy jeans—grungy in a different way than the ones on sale in Old Town.

"It depends," Andy says.

She rubs her eyes. "What day is this, anyway?"

"Friday."

"Wow. What happened to Thursday?" She takes a step closer and pretty much whispers, "So . . . ?"

Andy nods his head. "I'll catch up with you." When she's out of earshot, he says, "What a wastoid."

"Since when?"

"Since Charlotte Silano fell off Trigger. They were tight. Jill used to stay at Charlotte's house for like days when her mom brought some guy home. So when Charlotte got hurt, Jill kind of went downhill."

"Stop selling to her."

The shrug. "If I don't, somebody else will."

"That's a stupid thing to say."

"Did somebody I know skip breakfast, the most important meal of the day?" Andy's arm falls across my shoulder like a yoke. Which makes me the ox. Or the ass.

We walk toward the metal detector with Terence Patterson. Every day the guards hassle him. Every day they wave that wand up and down while he stands there. They even pull the chopstick out of his long, wadded-up hair, which makes him look like a girl with a beard. He's wearing paratrooper boots, camo pants, and a T-shirt with a mammoth drawn on the front with a Sharpie. Underneath that are two words: ASK ME.

Andy points. "So I'm asking."

Terence says, "You've seen the mammoths, right? They're all over town. Who do you think's doing that? Men in black cars, that's who. At midnight. The government wants us to be scared. Then we won't notice gas is nine bucks a gallon and the ice caps are melting. Those guys are the real monsters."

Andy taunts him, "Why don't you go chain yourself to another tree?"

"I just might do that."

We watch Terence stride away. "The tree-huggers think he's cool," Andy says. "Can you imagine trying to eat a hoagie and listening to that environmental bullshit?" Just then the bell rings. "I'll see you after school."

I shake my head. "I can't stand myself today."

"What?"

"I can't stand myself. I'm just going to go to the hospital."

"For what, a personality transplant?"

"For Charlotte."

"Holy shit, Ryan. Tell me you're not thinking that when she wakes up she's going to be all grateful."

"At least I'm doing something."

"Babysitting an almost-dead girl?"

"Don't say that! She's just in a coma. And at least I'm not selling drugs."

My accusations bounce off him. He's like Gulliver and I'm some inch-high archer with rubber-tipped arrows. He musses up—tries to muss up—my hair. "You don't get it, homey. Your mommy gives you money. What am I gonna do—work at McDonald's?"

After school, on the bus ride, I listen to John Lee Hooker's "Tupelo" and think about what the elements could do to me if they wanted to: burn me, drown me, bury me, blow me away. Weather could have put Charlotte in Saint Mary's if a breeze made her horse shy. Weather could have killed my sister—the rain that poisoned the lettuce, covering it with carcinogens.

On the lawn that stretches away from the hospital's big sliding doors, those soft places that looked like footprints are bigger. If there was only a pile of ape shit, I'd know King Kong had been here. He was a fool for beauty, so he'd like Charlotte.

In the hospital waiting room downstairs, a man watches one of those funny home-video shows. Thirty minutes of people falling down and running into things. The lady two seats away knits as fast as she can.

On Charlotte's floor I pass the nurses' station. Two glance up; only Monica smiles.

"Anybody down there?" I ask.

"Not right this minute."

Thad's at the window in his room. Today's hospital gown has pollywogs on it. He's wearing his Samuel L. Jackson hat. His arms are super-thin. When I walk up beside him, he blurts, "You don't believe me, do you? About Deadville."

"Get to the point, kid. Stop beating around the bush."

He grins and says, "Do you?"

"My mom's on your side. Or at least her yoga teacher is."

"Cool! What'd he say?"

"Pretty much what you did: waiting room, maybe go into the light, maybe come back."

"I told you, Ryan."

A nurse comes through the door with some things on a tray. Nothing to eat, either. Thad looks at her, the tray, then me.

"This isn't going to be fun."

"I'll catch you later."

He puts his arms around me, which makes me remember he's just a kid. Molly hugged everybody good-bye.

Next door Charlotte looks the same. There's a new balloon or two, and most of the old ones sag. Someone has put lipstick on her. Her mom, maybe. Molly wanted her fingernails painted, so Mom would do that. Molly never stopped liking the world. It made me sick to my stomach. In a way, the marijuana I smoked was medical.

I scoot closer in the hard-backed chair. I say, "Listen. I saw Jill this morning, and she's not doing too good without you. Okay? So there's another reason for you to come back."

She shudders. One of the articles I Googled told me that might happen, so I know it doesn't mean anything. People like her do that. People in comas. I'm glad I know, or I'd be pushing every button in the room.

I tell her, "You missed the Earthquake Preparedness assembly. If you weren't already in a coma, you would be after that. Oh, and the water polo team beat Blair three–zip. Not that I care, but you might."

The room is slightly familiar now — all the machinery, the flowers and balloons, the bag of urine. A slightly familiar neighborhood. Well, at least this time I could stay for a little while and not get stoned. The shape of that was still there, though. The need or desire. But only the shape. Like a ghost nobody would be afraid of.

When somebody knocks on the open door, I look up and there's Betty, who asks, "What are you doing here, Ryan?"

"Keeping Charlotte company. Somebody has to. You were so freaked out yesterday, I didn't think I'd ever see you again."

She strides toward me. "That's the point. I don't like to be freaked out. I'm a jock, okay? I don't backpedal. I go right at things."

"So this is like 'Get back on the horse'?"

"Ironic, isn't it. But, yeah. Just leave me alone, okay? I know what I'm doing."

Betty pretends I'm not there. I watch her frown and check things out. Or rather set things straight. First she lines up some more "Get Well" cards that somebody taped to the wall. Then she moves the water pitcher so the lip is facing the glass. She throws away some really droopy flowers, then empties the water into the toilet.

When that flushes with a roar, I glance at Charlotte. A sound like that would wake me up in a second.

I see Betty's in the middle of some deep, inner negotiations. Her outfit reflects her inner self—black from head to toe even if her high-tops are slightly frivolous. If she'd been playing volleyball, she'd be on the side of Darkness.

I don't move as she roams the room, one strap of her black tank top slipping off a muscled shoulder.

Then she focuses on Charlotte. Betty pushes back a few strands of hair, rubs the arm nearest her (us, actually), then pats her hand, all the time being careful of the IV. She's braver than I am. I still can't touch Charlotte.

After a minute or so, Betty goes to the window, digs in the pocket of her tight jeans. Whatever is there is folded up, but not in half. More like one of those pointy paper airplanes that kids make, the kind that never fly. She flattens it out on the windowsill, then angles the paper into the light so it's easier to read.

Finally she mutters, "Goddamnit."

"So much for prim."

"Like Elton knows anything." She inspects me. "You're not high, are you?"

"No."

"And you're not going to get high?"

"No."

"Why do I think I can trust you?"

"Beats me. Nobody else does."

She's undeterred. Not that I was trying to deter her.

She shows me. "This is a goddamned birthday card."

I look at the bear and the horsey and tell her, "It's for a little kid."

"My own mother doesn't know how old I am. It's not even my birthday. Granddad says I need to be ruthless and cut her out of my life."

I look at Charlotte. This isn't the upbeat talk the Internet said might help the comatose, but maybe Charlotte likes these kinds of bad tidings.

I ask, "Why don't you?"

"I don't know. I throw the envelope away and then go dig it out of the trash and write her back. Every time it's a different address in a different city. And listen to this—my mother calls my grandparents, they get the money together for rehab, she stays there awhile, then comes home and the next morning she's gone and so's the TV."

Why is she telling me any of this? Yesterday I was just this stoner at the bus stop, a guy she wanted nothing to do with.

"And if that wasn't enough," Betty says, "Patty Dean called me up again." She pounds both fists tenderly on her thighs. "She is so endlessly beguiled." She turns a raptor's eye on me. "What are you smiling about?"

"*Beguiled.* It's the kindest way to describe Patty Dean I've ever heard."

"You should know. You made out with her."

"Once. Up at the Flats. She'd just been scorned and didn't want to be by herself."

Betty's laugh is as sharp as a pistol shot. "'Scorned.'"

"Now we're even."

She plants both fists on her hips, Peter Pan style. "Who are you, anyway?"

She doesn't expect an answer. In fact, she turns on her heel and does something I've never seen a girl do. She goes into the bathroom and drinks from the tap. I can only see part of her, but I know what she's doing. She either wraps her lips around the faucet or laps at the trickling water like a dog.

Then she stands at the door and wipes her mouth with the back of one hand like a cowboy. "I feel better."

"Good."

A knock on the door makes us look up. Standing there is Jason Gamalinda, an eleventh-grader who drives a yellow Xterra. Kind of behind him is a girl about ten who's just got to be his sister. He's lean and wiry and suntanned but not in a golden Coppertone way. More like he's just been outdoors a lot.

"Am I interrupting something here?" Jason asks.

"Come on in. What's up?"

Jason takes a step into the room. His sister tries to hang back, but he won't let her.

"Jo Ann here wants to put a holy card in Charlotte's room."

Betty and I look at each other. She's the one who says, "Okay, I guess."

"Can I be by myself?" Jo Ann says. "I won't touch anything."

Her dress is long and blue, her collar little and white. She looks pious.

Out in the hall, Jason says, "Two months ago she was speaking Elvish. I hope she grows out of this . . . whatever it is."

I let the two of them drift ahead of me while I look in on Thad, who's asleep. He seems littler somehow. He's back in his baseball hat again, and it fits him like a saucepan fits a grapefruit.

By the time I catch up with Betty, she and Jason are in the lounge. He's really put together. His shorts are some kind of super-rugged material and his shirt is tight, but not just show-off tight. More so it won't catch on anything while he's climbing or riding his mountain bike. He makes me feel lazy and soft.

I wander over and stand by the snack machines. The peanut butter and Ritz crackers look about two hundred years old. Andy could eat a dozen packs of those things like it was nothing.

I hear Jason ask Betty, "How's your grandma?"

"Good."

"I remember her from grade school. She was playground monitor, right?"

"She likes kids. Not that hers turned out so well."

Just then Jason spots Jo Ann and waves her toward us. I like it that he's always got his eye out for her. I was like that with Molly. Not that she was careless or dumb or anything. She was just young and needed looking after.

Jo Ann is serious. She's got a mouthful of braces and one reverent expression. "Thank you," she says, "very much."

"Well," says Andy, waddling toward us. "The gang's all here."

I watch him and Jason do the NBA-MTV-soul-brother-hug-and-bump.

"What are you doing here?" Betty asks.

"I came for the meat loaf. There's nothing like hospital meat loaf."

Jason cackles, taps his fist with Andy's, then mine. His other arm goes around his sister's shoulders. "We're outta here. Time for me to ride a few hundred klicks. See you, Betty."

"Wait, wait," Betty says. "I'll go with you. I don't think Charlotte needs a crowd."

Andy stands for the kind of world her mother probably lives in. Why would Betty hang around? Which makes me kind of sorry Andy showed up.

"That guy climbs rocks," Andy says when they're out of earshot. "What's the point of that? And what was he doin' up here, anyway?"

"He brought his little sister by to see Charlotte."

"Well, I'm here. I might as well take a look. Which way?"

I point; he takes a step and loses his balance a little. He leans on the wall with this stupid grin on his face. I take one look at his eyes and ask, "Did you get high on your way over?"

"Do you think I'm crazy? I was driving. I got high in the parking lot."

"You've got to watch out for security around here."

"That old fart downstairs in somebody else's uniform? Get serious." He pushes himself onto both feet. "So where's the body?"

I walk him to room 531. Andy's T-shirt has a big smiley face on it, but his black baseball cap with the pentagram is from the Anarchist's Boutique.

Andy walks around the bed, taking it all in: Charlotte, tubes, monitors, bags—the whole coma package. Then he says, "Well, she doesn't look like Miss Hot Shit now, does she?"

So we stand there for a minute, both of us staring at Charlotte. All we need is a lily, some gloomy organ music, and a guy in a black suit. Finally Andy says, "So when's the caterer get here?"

I point to the upside-down bottle hanging next to her bed.

Andy scowls. "Talk about meals on wheels. Let's get outta here."

"I've only got about an hour."

Andy stops pouring himself a glass of water from the pitcher Charlotte never uses. "An hour. I thought we were gonna do something."

I shake my head. "I gave up and said I'd go to the gym with my dad."

He puts the glass down and slops some water onto the floor, barely missing Charlotte. "A gym?"

"I have to."

Andy squints and turns the bill of his hat sideways. It gives him a weird, off-kilter look. "I fronted you thousands of dollars' worth of ganja, man."

"And?"

"I want to do something."

"How'd we get from a simple 'I can't this time' to such a huge betrayal? You want to do quid pro quo? How about the thousands of dollars' worth of Double-Doubles and super-size everything?"

He takes a step back. "'Quid's bro's crow'? What are you talkin' about? I only got a C-plus on that paper you wrote for me. Fuck you, smart guy."

I point to Charlotte. "Watch your language, okay?"

Andy's mouth hangs open a little. He looks down at his hands like they're not his. "I'm goin', man. If you want a ride anywhere, I'm goin'."

I shake my head. "I'm going to stay with Charlotte."

SIX

On Monday I go to our usual table and put down my two mounds of cottage cheese and a bowl of mixed vegetables. The sound in the cafeteria is like a machine shop: a steady roar punctuated by the squeal of unlubricated things.

Minutes later Andy settles across from me and starts to eat. Not with his usual steam-shovel regularity, though. More like a series of badly timed twitches. Chunks of tamale pie fall off his fork.

"You okay?" I ask.

He concentrates on getting the food to his mouth. "I was up, like, all night killing zombies."

One of the Dead series, probably. I spent hours playing those games—one level after another. Never very good, just distracted by a highly pixilated city of the dead, a suburb of the dead, or just a whole bunch of the evil dead. Things I had some control over.

Just then, up comes marathon gamer Kyle Sisko with his big Buddy Holly glasses, tiki shirt, and black-and-white kicks.

"Guess who almost got to three million points in Pac-Man?" asks Andy.

"I missed a few blue ghosts," Kyle admits as he sets down his tray.

Andy nudges him. "Show him that storyboard you worked up, man."

"It's just a drawing." Kyle arranges the food on his tray—burger, milk, brownie. The bun is so perfect that it doesn't look real.

Andy has two helpings of tamale pie, salad, milk, cake. He points to my tray and asks, "Cottage cheese for lunch? What are you, a secretary?"

"Nothing else looked good to me."

"How's what's-her-name?"

"I know you're still pissed at me, Andy."

"I'm not pissed. I'm just busy. Kyle and I are working on this game called . . . what's it called, Kyle?"

"Reentry. It's one of those over-the-shoulder types where the player sees what Lydia sees."

"Lydia's great!" Andy crows. "Leather boots, leather

shorts, halter top. And she's got all kinds of secret weapons in her sorcerer's handbook."

"She's been to the Land of the Dead," Kyle says, "and she's trying to get back to this world."

"Kyle can really draw, can't you, man?"

"I can draw a little."

"A little! Man, you are great!"

Kyle touches one finger to his glasses, pushing them back up onto the bridge of his nose, where they belong. "What's up with you, man? Do I have to tell you to step away from the espresso machine?"

"I'm just stoked about Reentry is all. I want to call up that 3DO dude and pitch this baby."

"The pitch meeting is a long way away, Andy."

"He liked you, man. He gave you his card."

"I'm pretty sure he gave a lot of people his card."

I open a little packet of pepper and aim some at my cottage cheese, so now it looks like snow with soot on it. Andy and I used to play this video game set in a polar wasteland where a dead soldier's soul leaked out through his eyes. And then if you didn't shoot the soul, it animated the nearest monster and got right back in the game.

"Where'd you meet this 3DO guy?" I ask rather than think about migrating souls.

"Montreal. At this big gamers' convention. For a suit, he was pretty down-to-earth. He told me, 'You need three-dimensional maps; you want real characters compared to just realistic; and your player always needs to know where he is, where he should go, and how to get there. But basically never forget that people love to blow shit up.'"

"And I guess Lydia does that."

Kyle nods, takes a plastic knife, and divides his burger exactly in half. "Big time. It's not easy getting back from the Land of the Dead."

I remember when you were sick at home, before you went to the hospital for good, Mom would come into your room and close those shutters one at a time, so the room sort of got darker in pieces. Then I'd play George Harrison's "The Inner Light," the B-side to "Lady Madonna." Not that it was that great a song, but you didn't want it to feel left out.

"Ryan?"

It's Betty Bennett. I halfway get to my feet, which makes me semi-polite.

She says, "You were talking to yourself."

I glance around. Kyle and Andy are sketching something on a napkin. I point to my earphones. "I guess I was kind of singing along."

She sits down beside me. "Thursday was weird, wasn't it."

It's not a question, but I nod.

She says, "I'm okay now."

"You were okay Thursday. It was just one of those days."

She takes a spoon off my tray and samples the cottage cheese, which is the most intimate thing a girl has ever done to me or with me, and that includes the frenzied but anonymous making out with Patty Dean. "I was wondering," she says, "if you're going to go by Saint Mary's after school."

"I thought I might."

She leans in so only I can hear, and I smell talcum powder or soap. Nothing fancy. "Is Andy going to be there?"

I shake my head and tell her, "As Neil Sedaka said in nineteen sixty-two, 'Breaking up is hard to do.'"

"You are the oddest guy." She sits back. Her bracelet is silver and turquoise, probably something her grandparents bought for her. Something she might have hidden when her useless mother showed up.

Getting to her feet, she says, "I hope I see you at the hospital."

She has a long stride and a scab on one elbow (the right), probably from diving for a volleyball.

All of a sudden, Andy stands up and some of the stuff on his tray slides off onto the floor. "Good thing Charlotte Silano fell off her horse when she did, man. You never had so many friends."

. . .

109

When I pass the nurses' station after school, somebody I don't know glances up, nods, then down again. Monica must be working the night shift. She said that might happen.

Thad is propped up on his bed so that he can look out. When Molly was here, I saw a lot of sick kids. If I didn't know life wasn't fair before, I sure did then. Like with Thad. He's not supposed to be here. He's supposed to be playing ball and aggravating his parents.

"Hey."

I turn in. Thad holds up one hand, and I slap it in a kind of powder-puff way. Thad looks even thinner.

He closes his magazine, an old Bugs Bunny comic but in very good condition.

"I saw Charlotte today," he says. "Here, I mean. Not in Deadville. When they brought me back from my nine thousandth blood test, I looked in. She's the same. Her mom was praying like she always does."

"Seriously?"

"Every morning. Then she goes to work. She's pretty."

"I didn't know she did that."

"Prayed? Oh, yeah. Eight to ten. Nonstop."

I shake my head. "Man, I wish that worked." I prayed a lot when Molly was in this same hospital.

Just then some guy in a purple FedEx jacket knocks on the door and walks right in.

Thad grins. "This is my dad."

He's wiry-looking with a little mustache. I tell him my name, and we shake hands. Thad's busy drawing a tic-tac-toe grid on a pad of paper.

He warns me, "And don't help him, Ryan. I'm already down three–two from yesterday."

I really like it that there's a laptop, a PlayStation, and an iPod about four feet away, and they're using ballpoints and scratch paper. I watch Thad lose, and he groans like it really matters.

His father asks, "Ryan, you want to play the winner?"

"Thanks, no. I ought to look in on my friend next door."

He says, "Thad told me about her." He shakes his head. "Man, if it isn't one thing, it's another."

I'm on my way out when he leans into Thad, grabs him by the back of the neck, and kisses him hard on the forehead. "Your mom and I love you, kiddo. You know that, don't you?"

Charlotte's room has got new curtains. From her mother, probably. How sad is that—decorating your kid's hospital room. Mom did it for Molly, and it just killed me: Molly wanted her favorite shoes and her pink backpack, too, so we brought those and the stuffed shark she liked to sleep with.

Charlotte has a new 80 GB iPod on the nightstand.

I'm curious, so I hit Play and put one of the foamy cups up to my ear. The voice is quiet, like somebody talking in a museum. But a little fed up, too:

I can't believe you don't want to go skiing with your mom and me. You were getting really good right toward the end of the season. Remember that North Face jacket you got for Christmas? It's back from the cleaners and waiting for you. Come home and try it on. You'll get your strength back, and we'll go to the mountains. I'll take some vacation days.

I turn off the iPod and put the earphones on the table. I say, "Listen to your dad. It's good advice. Wake up and go skiing! You might have a choice, okay? And maybe the light looks better. But it's way too early for that. You're way to young to go there."

I hit the Play button again: *Your mother and I were just talking about that float trip on the Kern. That was fun, remember? Those class-four rapids were just scary enough. You and I hiked away on our own and went swimming. That water was so cold, but the rocks were warm. We could do that again, honey.*

What if I was in a coma? My parents would come to visit me, or at least my mom would. But what about kids from school? Andy'd drop by a time or two, and then he'd bring Kyle up from the minors. Betty might come, but not for long. We could like each other, I think, but we don't yet. Not really.

I'm on my feet stretching when Charlotte's father comes in, and I'm really glad I wasn't still listening to that secret recording he made for her.

He's in green scrubs and running shoes. He looks more like an outfielder than a doctor. "I'm Charlotte's dad." Then he looks around. "You the only one here?"

"Yeah."

I remember him from that first day when Charlotte was in the ICU and he walked in with his wife.

I point. "I recognize you from the pictures."

"Do you know Charlotte from school?" the doctor asks.

"Sort of." I'm slightly embarrassed that my T-shirt says SLAYER.

"But you're not in her class, are you?"

I shake my head and step back. He goes past me, kisses his daughter like a prince in a story, whispers something, brushes at her bangs. I'm careful not to stare.

He says, "The nurses tell me you've been a pretty regular visitor."

"I, uh, just came with some of the other kids right after the accident . . . Then kind of didn't for a while . . . And then I started again. I tell her stuff about school mostly. We didn't . . ." I almost say, ". . . hang out or any-thing." But he knows that.

Both hands come out of his pockets, and he crosses his arms. "I don't get it."

"What's there to get?"

He scowls. "Were you ever at the house for a pool party or something like—"

"Look, if you don't want me to come, I won't."

"I didn't say that. I'm just trying to . . . Monica says you're okay. You and . . . There's a girl sometimes, right?"

"Betty."

"If Monica thinks you can be alone with her, I guess I do, too."

Oh, that. "You think I'm some kind of perv?"

"It happens."

"You ran with my dad. He's a runner. He said he knew you."

"What's your name?"

"Glazier. Ryan Glazier."

"Oh, yeah. Robert, right? Tall, skinny guy from JPL."

"He might be skinny, but he buried your ass after three miles."

He looks half mad. I guess he's had these interviews before when platoons of suitors came to his front door. That was over—it was ritualistic, anyway. She would never go out with somebody he didn't approve of—but now he had to stumble through it with me under these gruesome circumstances.

"I still don't get it, but maybe I don't have to." He gives me a look that says, "Watch your step." Then he turns away fast.

From the back, Dr. Silano fills out his green scrubs. Broad shoulders, thirty-two inch waist. A shaved head that's not smooth all over.

His life was one way (skiing, rafting), then his daughter falls off a horse and it's another. Like mine after Molly.

He makes it to the door, then stops, looks at Charlotte, and recites, "Her brain activity is fine. She's never been on a ventilator. She's always breathed on her own. There's no medical reason she shouldn't be awake. That's one of the reasons we don't move her. I don't want to change anything." He glances at his watch. "She's a fighter. She'll come back."

Once he's gone, I sit down in the chair beside her bed. "Did you hear that?" I ask. "Fight a little harder, okay?"

Just then Betty peeks in the door and says, "You're here."

She's all dressed up. Or at least dressed different. Everything looks ironed. Real shoes versus sneaks. I tell her, "You look nice."

"I hoped one of you would notice." Betty turns toward the door. "I just saw Charlotte's dad."

"Yeah, he thinks I'm feeling up his daughter when nobody else is around."

Betty blushes just a little. "He doesn't know you."

"He knows you, though."

"From the house. We'd go there after games and stuff."

"The famous pool parties."

"Sometimes."

"And you vouched for me."

"I told him I know you and you're nice."

Nice. When's the last time anybody said that about me?

Betty points to the player on the table by Charlotte's bed. "What's she listening to?"

"Stuff from her dad. Basically, 'Please come back.'"

Betty points to the pocket where I keep my iPod. "What about you?"

"Um, the Hold Steady."

"Can I?"

I hand her the earbuds. "Now I can concentrate on ravishing Charlotte."

"He's just being careful." She holds up one finger, which means "shut up so I can listen." Then she says, "I like these guys."

I like this conversation. It's down-to-earth. She says something, then I say something back. "You know them?"

"Sure."

"Seriously?"

"No. I was just running the movie: Boy meets girl, he's into music, she knows some semi-obscure band, he's impressed, they go to the beach and hold hands, she jumps on his back, they horse around, then fall down in the sand and make out. Except I don't actually know the semi-obscure band. And it's a stupid movie, anyway." She slips past me, picks up Charlotte's hand, and pats it. "She's pretty."

"She was always pretty."

"Not like she is now. She could guard the gates of paradise."

Betty's hair is red or reddish. She wears a lot of green. Like today—avocado-colored pants. Narrow ones because she's tall and strong-looking. Is everybody in better shape than me?

"What gates of paradise?" I ask.

"You know, you die and go to heaven, and there's Charlotte all pale and mysterious hovering around the door. Who'd be surprised?"

"Do you believe in that stuff?"

"What stuff?" she asks.

"You know—pearly gates, Saint Peter. That kind of stuff."

"Probably not. That's from Sunday school."

I stand up. "I'd better get home. This time Dad and I are supposed to actually get inside the gym."

She looks me up and down. "You go to a gym?"

"Don't be cruel. We're just getting started."

Betty walks me toward the door, then waits until a nurse goes by in her squeaky shoes. "You and I made Cynthia Wixen's blog. We're the Good Samaritan Couple of the Month."

"Who is she, anyway? Has anybody ever seen her?"

"Oh, yeah. Cynthia was in my health ed class." Betty draws a shape in the air. "She's kind of round and looks like she spends too much time indoors."

The black-and-white movie that's been muttering on Charlotte's TV gets replaced by a big, noisy ad for wrestling. I reach for the remote and the mute button.

Betty says, "I'm ashamed to say I know who Crippler Crossface is. Way too many Friday nights with my grandparents."

On the screen two steroid-addled poseurs throw it down. Then the movie comes back on. Guys in suits going into a nightclub and giving their coats and hats to a cute girl.

"Are you going to hang around?" I ask.

She points to the red purse still slung over one shoulder. "I've got a book in here. I'll read to her."

I'm almost through the door when she says, "I just finished this story where if you liked somebody or wanted to like him, you had to get permission from a Nearness Inspector."

I lean against the nearest wall. "And?"

"That's all. I just thought you might find that interesting."

SEVEN

A couple of nights later, I'm watching TV with my mom while we're waiting for Dad to get home. This morning there was nothing in the world that would keep us from the gym tonight, but he's already late. Again.

My mother says, "You look very nice in those clothes. Very athletic."

"Oh, please."

I watch the guys in this movie lay their hats on the hall table or hang them on racks or give them to somebody behind a counter. I like the cut of their suits and their shiny shoes.

Just then Mom's cell buzzes, so she talks to Mr. Vega and giggles. I wish she wouldn't do that while I'm around.

When the landline rings, I pick up.

"I'm stuck here," my dad says. "Just tell your mother not to wait up."

When I put the phone down, my mom looks at me and asks, "What's up?"

"Dad said for you marry Mr. Vega and move to Arizona."

She says into her cell, "Let me call you back." Then she looks at me. "What'd he really say?"

"That he's stuck at the lab." I point at myself. "And here I am in this lame outfit."

"You should go by yourself."

I shake my head. "No way. This is his stupid idea."

Mom stands up and brushes something invisible off her shirt. "Take my car."

That stops me. "Really?"

She gives the keys a toss. A bad one. But I catch them with the side of my shoe, then snatch them out of the air. It wasn't even something I tried to do. My body just remembered. So *I* didn't have to go to the gym; I could just take my body there.

"Follow through with something," she says. "For a change."

Twenty minutes later I pull into the Weight World parking lot and just sit there. A couple of older guys come out with their comb-overs in place, then three gals (that's what my mom calls her friends). When they walk past the car, I hear one of them say, "And I'm supposed to think that's just peachy?"

I feel sixteen. Somebody's kid who either had to go to the gym because his parents told him to or was just here on his own after one too many Bowflex commercials at 4:00 A.M. In other words, nobody was going to pay any attention to me.

On the way in, I wait for a silver Lexus with a huge sound system to turn off its headlights. Two guys bust out of it like bank robbers and blow by me.

One of them points. "What's all that about?"

His friend looks up and says, "The mammoth? Carpe diem, man. Before it's too late."

I take a deep breath and climb the steps. My new sneaks are white as bunnies. Some guy pushes the door way wide for me, which means "I know you're there, but I'm not going to hold this open like some candy-ass."

But before I can step inside, a little girl about three, who's standing by her mom at the counter, bolts for the parking lot. I drop my gym bag, reach out with my right hand, and grab her. The momentum carries us in a half-circle.

"Erica!"

Her mom is right there, tugging at her, but Erica has

both arms around my neck. Her breath smells like the best snacks in the world. She's looking at me. Into me. Her eyes are green, the white part like Communion candles.

Her mom tugs at her and apologizes. "I'm so sorry. She's usually not like this. Erica!"

"It's fine." I pry at her arms, but halfheartedly. First, I don't want to hurt her. Second, nobody has put her arms around me with this much enthusiasm for a long time.

Erica's mom has her hair teased into points. "Honey. The man is coming in with us. He'll be right there. Won't you be right there?"

"Sure."

Finally she lets go, and we walk in together. Erica's mom finishes what she started at the desk. She smiles at me, then heads for a glassed-in room full of colored balls and toys. A big sign says CHILD CARE. Erica doesn't care; she won't take her eyes off me.

The music is loud. It's Sugababes' "About You Now." A gaggle of spandex goddesses behind the counter bob and sway.

"Can I help you?" This one must be the Muse of Lip Gloss.

"Um. Yeah. My last name is Glazier, but I haven't been here before."

"I'll be right with you."

There must be twenty-four stair-steppers along one of

the glass walls that look out onto Myrtle Avenue. Another two dozen treadmills and stationary bikes, and a guy could break his neck getting around all the other machines with levers, pulleys, bars, chains, ropes, and belts. This is nothing like that lame gym at school with one trampoline and a climbing rope.

She taps on the nearest computer. "I'm Mitzi. Are you Ryan or Robert?"

"I'm Ryan. Robert's not coming. There's a crisis on the moon."

"Let me see who's up next."

There aren't any back pockets in my new pants, so I don't know what to do with my hands. By the north windows, people climb to nowhere. Some of them read magazines and cruise; others hang on the bars and dog it.

"Rhett," says the trainer, pointing to his name tag. "And before you ask, yes. It's Rhett like in *Gone with the Wind,* but we both know it's better that than Ashley."

He's forty or so—broad shouldered, kind of balding. But strong-looking with big biceps. He pulls on my T-shirt and leads me toward a scale. "Stand over here; let me take a look at you."

I volunteer some information. "I used to play sports, but not for, like, two years."

"Did you hurt yourself?"

"I just picked up some bad habits, I guess."

"Here's the drill, Ryan. Keep some celery and carrots in the fridge. Whatever else you want to eat, don't. It's behavior modification, nothing more."

I wait for a girl to go by in a SPAM T-shirt—the blue can, the yellow letters. Then I confess, "It wasn't just food."

Rhett just shrugs. "Doesn't matter. If X is what got you into the shape you're in now, do Y instead. I'm not saying it's easy. I'm just saying it's simple." He glances at an index card in his hand. "How's this for a plan: Lose some weight and firm up. I don't see you power lifting or doing low reps/high weight. You're tall enough to go for lean and mean."

Or keen and seen. Or clean and green. But I say, "Sure."

He puts one hand on my shoulder and guides me. "Muscle weighs more than fat. You might not need to lose a ton, but you can drop a few belt notches while you redistribute things." He turns away, answers a question from one of the goddesses, then says to me, "Let's get you warmed up. The rowing machine's free. Is that okay, or do you want to wait for a bike?"

"Whatever."

I follow him to the southwest corner, weaving around the equipment and the people groaning and straining and panting. There's a lot of flirting going on but not with other people. *How do I look?* And the mirror says, *Wonderful. Never better.* Or maybe, *You slob. You'll never amount to anything.*

Rhett leads me over to this long, low machine that looks like a bad idea for a boat. "It's a terrific device," he says. "Upper and lower body, cardio, the whole package. And once you get a rhythm going, it's very Zen-like."

He points out a couple of things, then gets on and shows me: "Push *and* pull," he says. "Let the legs do a lot of the work. Back straight. Don't hunch over."

It's harder than it looks. I've got a lot of hand-to-lip coordination, thanks to Andy and his atomic blunts. This kind, not so much.

"Slow down," Rhett says. "It's not a race. I'll be back in fifteen," he says. "And take it easy, okay?"

I look at my legs; they're as soft as all the muffins Andy and I ate. At least I'm using them. At the hospital the PT guy has to come in and move Charlotte's legs for her.

I wonder what Betty's doing.

"Kiss."

I glance up and there's Erica. She points at my cheek and says it again. "Kiss."

I spot her mom coming our way at top speed, so I stall for time. "Long time, no see, kiddo. How was the playroom?"

Her mom scoops her up and says, "I am so sorry. She

opened the door by herself and just . . . I don't know. She's usually not like this."

Erica's wailing away, kicking her little heels, pounding with her little fists. Her mom tries carrying her like a torpedo, but Erica squirms free, lands running, and is right next to me in three seconds flat.

"Kiss."

"If you wouldn't mind," her mom says. "Just . . . let her. She gets attached to a word. This week it's *kiss*."

So I lean and say, "Just one."

Her arms go around my neck. She collides with my cheek, then steps back looking proud of herself. She's wearing blue shorts and a yellow top with LAKERS written across it at an angle.

I tell her, "Go play some more. I'll say good-bye, okay?"

All of a sudden, she's docile and shy. It was like she melted and reconstituted into somebody else. A different little girl.

Ten minutes later Rhett wants to show me how to use the rest of the equipment—a couple kinds of bench presses, pull-ups and dips, lat pull-downs, biceps curls, triceps extensions.

"Just get a feel for everything, okay? Keep moving. Don't rest between sets. This is partly strength and muscle tone, partly cardio. I want your heart rate in the zone."

There's a little line at the silver fountain. I take a turn and get out of the way. Somebody about my dad's age slurps, lets the water hit him in the face, then wets both hands and runs them through his hair. His face is long and vulpine, he's got hair sprouting out of his tank top, and he looks like he could run forever. Molly and I used to play Wolfman. I'd lope, and she'd chase me with a toy gun and a pretend silver bullet. Then I'd let her catch me. I'd fall to my knees and sob, "Don't shoot me. Tomorrow I'll be a normal boy again!"

I try the machines, then some free weights. Light ones. And I see what Rhett meant when he said the machines make a guy mindless. The dumbbells need looking after. Otherwise they wobble and sway. I like my mind to think about my muscles. On the machines it wanders.

Eventually Rhett walks me toward the front, "Three times a week is best, okay? Remember—if X got you someplace you don't want to be, do Y. More rowing or running. Or both." He looks at his right arm. "Who needs big biceps like this? What good do they do?"

"So why do you bother?"

"I'm an alcoholic. When I want to reach for a Scotch, I pick up a dumbbell instead."

"You could run."

He shakes his head. "It doesn't hurt enough."

We shake hands. I look into the playroom, but Erica

is busy pounding on a ball with a rubber mallet. Her indifference shakes me a little.

In the parking lot, I call my mom. "I'm going to go by the hospital."

Of all the things she could have said—and those are "Fine" or "Are you all right?" or "Don't be too late"—what she does say is the most unexpected: "Take me. I'll be out front. You'll barely have to slow down."

"So, how was it?" She buckles the seat belt and sits back.

"The gym? Kind of hard."

"Will you go back?"

I look both ways before I turn, then answer. "I think so. Yeah."

"Take your dad. He'll never go on his own."

"Well, sure. Who wants to show up all by himself in cruelty-free sneaks and an organic jock strap?"

The conversation we aren't having goes on under this one, like subtitles that don't match the movie. Something's going on. I just don't know what yet.

When a beater passes us with its radio blaring, I say, "I thought for a minute that was Andy."

"Don't talk to me about Andy. What's he going to do with his life, anyway?"

I slow down a little. "He says he's gonna travel, for one thing. He says he might go to Alaska after graduation."

Her laugh is composed of equal parts: disbelief/scorn. "How high is he when he tells you that?"

"Andy didn't make me do anything I didn't want to do."

"Don't remind me."

It's not late, but the streets are almost empty. I have a feeling we're going somewhere I don't want to go, and I don't mean the hospital. I turn the radio on and it's Karen Dalton. Mom sings along, ". . . and sleep out in the rain."

I tell her, "You should make a record."

"What happened at the gym?"

"What's with you? Nothing happened at the gym."

"You never go to the hospital at night. Something happened."

I can see Saint Mary's in the distance. There's a lot of bland-looking sky around, so it stands out like sarcasm.

"This little girl who was there with her mom reminded me of Molly, that's all. Why that would make me want to go to the hospital, I don't know. But it did."

"She reminded you of Molly when she was little?"

I nod. "Three, maybe. Really cute."

"Not like when Molly was twelve. A spoiled tween with a cell phone and her own credit card."

I check the road in front of me, then look at her a long time. "If you're going to talk like that, I'm taking

you home. And no ice cream when we get to the beach."
I'm kidding and I'm not.

"I just want to put an end to any idolatry that's lingering."

"Mom, I know she wasn't perfect. And shut up a minute, okay? While I park."

I find a place without a car on either side. I turn off the engine and listen to it tick. Mom taps the dashboard like she's sending Morse code. Then she asks, "What did you get from Molly's death?"

"Are you nuts?"

"What did you—"

"I'm not talking about this."

"I know it's a hard question, but I ask those. I don't run away from them like some chicken-shit JPL scientist we know."

I pretty much shout at her, "I didn't get anything from her death, all right? I hate it that she died. Happy now?"

"You had to get something, Ryan. You had to. Otherwise she just died." Her seat belt is loose, so she can scoot closer to me. "Listen to me. When people you love cross over, here's what happens: whatever you thought about life or the world or the way things are gets all turned upside down. You cry, you grieve, you say, 'How could this happen?' You're mad at God; you're mad at yourself. You're in some not-here-but-not-there zone, okay? Are you listening to me?"

I put my hands over my ears. "No."

"And then that's over and you come out on the other side. You've got scars, you're beat up, you're a different person, but you're through it." She motions. "Give me your hand."

"No."

"Give me your goddamned hand."

I really don't want to, but she grabs it. "I would die for you," she says. "You're my son and I love you. If somebody came up to this car with a gun right now and pointed it at you, I'd find a way to take the bullet. I told God in the hospital, 'Take me. Let Molly live.' No deal."

She's holding on to me so hard it hurts.

I can't stop myself from asking, "How can you say anybody got anything out of what happened?"

She pulls me toward her. "Look at what you're doing right now. Look at what you do every time you come to this hospital. Molly dies, your heart breaks, but two years later you're able to step up and help Charlotte Silano's family because you know what it's like to suffer."

I put my forehead on the steering wheel; I hear myself say, "Mama, don't." And I know how far I've sunk. All the way to Mamaland.

"You're something special," she says. "You just don't know it yet."

She lets me blubber and drip on her steering column. When she hands me a Kleenex, I push her hand away.

"What room is she in?"

I look up. "Five thirty-one. What are you going to do?"

"I just want five minutes alone with her."

"Some more of that bullshit you learned in yoga class?"

She opens the door. "Who needs your father around when I've got you." But she comes to my side of the car, anyway, leans in, and kisses me hard enough to leave a scar. "Don't go anyplace, tough guy," she says. "I'll be right back."

EIGHT

I sure don't feel special, and nothing special happens: I go to the gym three times a week, school five times a week, and I see Charlotte almost every day.

I do decide Mom is right and my T-shirts are more crummy than classic. So one day right after sixth period, I hop on a bus.

Aardvark's Vintage is big and kind of musty. The clerks are the usual Goth warlocks with lots of tattoos and piercings. Six or eight years older than me—a lifetime.

The last time I was in here was with Andy, and we were pretty wasted. Memory nudging me in the ribs with its sharp elbow.

I go up to the counter where two employees—all in black, of course—are almost lying down on the counter, like sunlight is sucking the life out of them. They're sharing an old iPod, hooked up to the music like an IV.

I ask, "What are you guys listening to?"

Wearily, one of them hands me the earbud. I take ten seconds and then say, "Girls Under Glass."

"Dude," he says. "What can I do for you?"

I point to my head. "Hats?"

"In the back."

Going to the gym makes me want my body to speak a different language. So I'd better dress it in the regional garb.

I pass a woman with tatts of her own and a dozen studs in one ear. Two or three different colored tank tops, a velvety-looking skirt, big kicks with steel toes. She's talking on her cell but folds that up abruptly and asks, "What can I help you with?"

I point. "Maybe one of those with a brim?"

"The felt one is a Bogart. Comes with a pack of cigarettes and a hangover." She grabs a medium-size pole and lifts that one down, then a couple more. "Try 'em on. I'll turn my back if you're shy." She holds out one hand. "Suzanne. I own this joint."

We both watch me in the mirror. "Hmmm," she says. "Pretty good. Now you need a pair of linen pants and a gin and tonic." She appraises me. "What are you— thirty-four waist?"

Suzanne is gone before I can say anything else.

"Ryan? What are you doing in here, man?"

It's Jason Gamalinda and Claire Caldwell. She has that out-of-jail look kids get around three thirty. She's thin with freckles sprinkled across her bare shoulders. Otherwise it's just flip-flops, cutoffs, and a tank top.

Jason leans toward me, and Claire looks the other way. I know what's coming. The cloak-and-dagger stuff. The password. "You wouldn't have a little Astroturf, would you?"

I shake my head.

"Try this," Claire says, and she holds up a shirt for me to try on. It's black with flames shooting up out of both pockets. She retreats, cocks her head, shakes it. "No. Too eager to please." She's got another one for me almost immediately. I like to watch her scan the racks. "Here we go."

Blue this time, plain except for an embroidered clock on the left sleeve.

"Just reined-in enough," she says as Suzanne appears with a pair of pants she holds right up against me.

"Plenty long, and perfect with the shirt." She squints, and I can tell she's doing math in her head. "Tell Sledge it's fifty-five for everything."

I kind of want to step into the mirror, into that guy there, and step back out as one person. Not two.

"A steal," says Claire. "If I wasn't with Jason, I'd jump your bones."

I wear the shirt and the hat, and take the pants in a bag. Outside we stand by a mannequin in a frilly dress. The window behind us is every color there is, and right at the bottom, just before the foundation starts, are four words: THE VANITY OF PROGRESS.

"The hat is very noir," Claire says.

Jason tells me, "Too many black-and-white movies. Everything's 'noir' with her."

"You're not."

"I'll see you guys."

He points to his car, a yellow Xterra with mud caked on the hubs. "We'll take you."

I shake my head. "I'm just going to Saint Mary's."

Claire squeals. "To see Charlotte? Can we come?"

"I told her I took Jo Ann." Jason is sheepish and apologetic.

"I guess. Why not? Sure."

The back of his SUV is dirty and cluttered with rock-climbing gear like helmets and carabiners and those skinny, sticky-soled shoes. He's tanned, and his arms—even holding the steering wheel—look strong. He's got the radio cranked up, so we couldn't talk if we wanted to. It's an old Sex Pistols CD. He probably plays it on his way to the rock face and then is so amped he just sprints up it.

I put the bag with the slacks in it beside Claire's school clothes and hold on. Everything's off-road to Jason, so when we get to the hospital, he blows by the ticket machine, shifts into four-wheel drive, climbs over the curb, then plows through some oleanders before he pulls right up to the entrance.

"Here you go," Jason says.

"This is so cool," says Claire. "I kind of knew Charlotte."

"Since when?" asks Jason.

"I was wearing these super low-rise pants and Charlotte asked me where I got them and I said Forever 21 and she said, 'Thanks.'"

Jason waves us out. "You take her. I'll park this buggy and meet you."

On our way in, I put on my hat so I can take it off in the elevator. Which I do once the doors slide open and I let Claire go first.

"I'll hold it for you," she says. She lifts the brim to her nose and sniffs. "Definitely vintage," she says as she puts it on.

It's huge and drops down over her eyes, which makes her laugh.

When the door opens, she puts her hand on my forearm. "Pretend I'm blind," she says.

"Take it easy."

She grimaces. "Sorry."

I tug on her, and we walk past a few closed doors. I wonder what's going on inside. Closed doors aren't usually a good sign. When I went to visit Molly and her door was closed, it freaked me out.

We stop at Thad's room. He's asleep, and it looks like there's a new tube leading to his arm. It could be anything: food, glucose, saline.

"That's not chemo," Claire says like she could read my mind. "They put up signs if it's chemo. My mom had it."

I tell her, "The kid in there says he can go to the other side, someplace called Deadville."

"Like high school?"

"More like a place to wait after you've been really sick or in an accident, but before you're really dead."

"Oh, yeah? A girlfriend of mine was online with this Buddhist priest, and he said that right after you die, you have to go through these bardos, which I think are like the projects or maybe the Haunted Mine at Six Flags. Anyway, you have to go through them, and if you do okay, you don't have to come back as a skank. But I don't know if I believe him, because he's the one who wanted a picture of her in a bikini."

I move us along. The door to 531 is wide open. "Here we are."

Claire goes right to her knees and makes the sign of the cross.

I tell her, "Don't do that."

She looks up at me. "Why not?"

"She's not a roadside attraction."

Claire gets to her feet. "Can I touch her? I don't know what I thought she'd look like. Can't they put her in the sun or something? Is it true that sometimes nurses bring sick babies in here and they get well?"

"Get serious."

"You're not here all the time. They could. My allergies are better already."

I think about getting high so I won't have to listen to her. Weed would muffle the electric carving knife of her voice, and we could all sit at the table in silence.

Just then Dr. Silano shows up and dismisses us like rumors. "I've got a couple of colleagues coming in."

He walks us toward the door and closes it after us.

"What's his problem?" Claire asks.

"He's just worried about Charlotte."

When the elevator comes, I ask her to hold the door for a second. "I need to call Betty. She was going to meet me here."

Betty picks up on the second ring.

"Don't come by the hospital," I tell her.

She says, "I'm already at the hospital, Ryan. I'm downstairs."

"Stay there. We'll be right down."

"Who's we?"

"Me and Claire Caldwell. Jason's supposed to be parking the car."

In the elevator Claire says, "Put your hat on so it's the first thing Betty sees."

I do, but by the time we get there, Jason's talking to Betty. He holds up his cell. "I got a call so I didn't come up," he says to Claire and me. "What's the plan?"

Betty says, "I guess I'll buy the cute guy with the hat a cup of coffee."

Claire pulls at Betty's sleeve. "Come to the Flats with us."

"Yeah," says Jason.

I shake my head. "No way."

Jason says, "It's not like that right after school. There's hardly anybody. Just you and nature. Claire and I go all the time to meditate and stuff, don't we, Claire?"

"All the time." She opens the back door. "C'mon, you guys."

I look at Betty, who shrugs. "I'm game if you are."

Jason's parked in the red but didn't get a ticket. We climb in, and he drives over the same oleanders and down the same curb, this time with a big *thunk*. Behind us a security guard yells. Claire turns on the radio, where somebody's rapping about how life's not fair, betrayal's in the air. I could never get into rap, but I liked a guy named Ghostface Killah for a while. Or I liked his name, anyway. A lot of his stuff didn't make sense, which in its own weird way was perfect.

Jason drives, and Claire lets her head rest on his shoulder. They're whispering and laughing. Betty and I look out the window as we head up toward the foothills. The last time I was on this street, Andy and I were shooting paintballs at Chris Teagarden's Mustang. I wasn't even high, just vengeful.

The neighborhoods look idle and bored. There's a lot of graffiti along the wall that separates federal land from the suburbs. A mammoth or two looking bewildered are among the huge, swooping runes and spells and counter-charms.

Claire turns around so she's on her knees facing us. "Ryan's got new pants, too."

I hold up the bag from Aardvark's.

Betty peeks in. "You know you're supposed to put them on, right? Not just carry them around."

Just before Jason turns off the two-lane road and heads into the trees, Betty asks him to stop for a minute.

"I better call my grandma, and the signal's lousy up there."

"Take your time," says Jason, "Claire and I will make out."

"You wish," says Claire. But she does it, anyway, though it seems perfunctory.

Betty and I get out of the car. She wanders toward the front fender; I wander toward the back.

While I'm waiting for my mom to pick up, I can hear Betty's side of the conversation. "I won't be home for dinner, but I won't be late. With this boy I told you about from the hospital. His dad's the JPL guy. I'll ask him. And I'll bring him by if we have time, okay?"

I know there are rites and duties associated with the sacrament of courtship, but a lot of kids don't bother with that anymore. They couple and uncouple like train cars in some dark and anonymous yard. I suspect I'm soon to experience one of those duties firsthand: meeting with the leaders of the clan.

So does this mean Betty and I are going together? Or have we been going together for a while, and I'm just too dumb to know? And if we are together, when exactly did that happen—one afternoon in Charlotte's room?

My mom doesn't pick up, so I talk to the answering machine.

Pretty soon we're up the road with trees all around us. We pass a few kids walking. Kids who have parked their mother's Volvo or Saab where it will be safe. A guy Jason knows is carrying half a dozen pizzas, so he hitches a ride by climbing onto the back bumper and holding on with one hand. If there is a deeper rut or a bigger rock that Jason can find, he drives in it or over it. So Betty and I are bouncing off each other. "Are you meditating yet?" I ask her.

She grabs the door handle with one hand and me with the other. "Not yet," she says.

"Have I seen you up here?"

"I don't come very much. I think about getting busted and then calling my grandparents to come get me, and my blood just runs cold."

"Why would you get busted? You don't smoke."

"Guilt by association, I guess."

After that we just hold on.

Finally Jason skids to a stop, and we all climb out.

The Flats. Lots of trees, an almost-dry stream, and enough of a level place to string a rope that passes for a volleyball net. My mom came up here when she was in high school. And I accompanied Andy on his many business trips.

Claire nudges me and points. "Check it out."

I take in the biggest boulder, where somebody has

crossed out "Jesus," so now the question is "What Would Charlotte Do?"

"Charlotte," says Betty, "would get her toenails done."

I say hi to a guy named Connor who always sports a tired-looking Mohawk.

"Hey, man," he says as he shuffles closer to me. "Is it true that Charlotte Silano's, like, vegetarian?"

His on-again-off-again girlfriend, one Tori Hallman, slaps him open-handed across the back of the head and says, "Vegetative, stupid."

"She's pretty much the same," I tell him. "But not worse."

"Did you, like, know her or something?" he asks.

"Not really."

Connor's got a small Tinker Bell tattoo on his neck. When he squirms and bobs his head, her little wand moves. "Then I don't get it," he says.

"What's to get?" I nudge Betty and we head downhill, helping each other to get to the splintery picnic tables, because we're walking on pine needles and rotting leaves, so the footing is precarious.

The Flats is arranged with corporate efficiency: Drugs, Alcohol, Food, Dalliance, Sports. By the time we get to the Food pavilion, and this may explain the mob scene, Derricotte is yelling for everyone to stand back. "Claire, when we're all set, you say go."

Claire nods as Derricotte hunches over the table piled up with pizza boxes. Beside him are his two linemen pals, Lehane and Johnston. Plus Andy.

Claire yells, "Go!"

I watch Andy fold up a major slice and shove it in his mouth.

"I know the Heimlich," Betty says. "But I don't want to have to give it to any of those guys."

We drift by a washtub where half a dozen Cokes in old-fashioned green glass bottles are standing logo-deep in murky water. Betty takes one anyway.

As we walk away, she says, "I guess I don't get it, either. What Conner said about Charlotte, I mean. You and Charlotte."

I stop, so she does, too. The hill is steep, so we have to stand at angles to keep our balance. "Why do *you* go?" I ask.

"Because you're there, Ryan Glazier. There's not another boy in this school or anywhere else for all I know who'd go to that hospital every day. Apparently altruism gets me hot."

I put my hand on her shoulder, and she leans into me. Now I know we are definitely going together.

I tell her, "I don't know if it's all that altruistic. I messed up when my sister was sick."

"Is that when you started getting high all the time?"

"I couldn't even get close to that hospital unless I was stoned."

The nearest place to sit down is at a long picnic table with Danny Mitchell and Jerry Fisher. Voc ed guys. Gear heads. Danny I've known since grade school. All he ever did was draw cars in his notebooks. He and Jerry are sitting at one end. They've both got a can of beer, and between them a bag of tortilla chips and a green carton.

"Hey, Ryan." Danny slides the green carton our way. "Want some of this?"

"What is it?"

"It's either guacamole or alien DNA."

Betty holds up one hand. "I'll pass on that."

Jerry turns to face us. "I was telling Danny here, I kind of want a gun."

I just look at him. It's such an unoriginal thing to say—a dream that's been pre-dreamed and tested for product placement: the door barred, the windows shuttered, Jerry bare chested and sweaty and armed to the teeth, a girl with lemonade-colored hair who depends on him. And—oh, yeah—a dog.

"The sign of the mammoth, man. Don't you listen to the news? Bird flu, killer viruses, Al-Qaeda, all that stuff. Okay, you can't shoot the virus, but you can shoot the guy who's got it. He wants your water, your jerky, and your woman."

"Just think," says Betty, "if I had water and jerky, I'd be the most popular girl at the Apocalypse."

Jerry picks up his beer. "Okay, but you won't think it's so funny when everything's on fire." And he heads toward the nearest barbecue pit with his feelings just a little hurt.

Betty puts her head against my shoulder. My mom has a book of sutras, which are kind of like Buddhist sermons. Some of them start with the same words—"In which." So if there was a Sutra of the Flats, it might go like this: In which he is caressed by her. In which he returns the caress tentatively. In which it occurs to him he has crossed some kind of border. In which things are different between them at least slightly. In which he realizes he does not know exactly what to do next.

Just then Danny's phone rings. He doesn't even say hello. "Mom, I'm fine. Pretty soon. Yes. Bottled water, and if I drink any more, the cops are gonna stop me for driving wet." He flips the phone closed and looks over at Betty and me. "Where's a hungry mammoth when you need one?" Danny starts down the hill, slips and falls, then gets up and checks to see if he's broken his phone.

"Hey, you guys." It's Derek, Charlotte's boyfriend. He puts his hand on my shoulder. "Ryan, can I talk to you for a minute?"

Betty looks up at him. "How's Sheila?"

Derek frowns. "Don't be like that."

Betty stands, kisses me on the check, and says, "I'm gonna see if there are two pieces of pizza left in the whole world."

Derek gives me this bogus smile. "Cool fedora."

"That's what I hear."

He really is a good-looking guy—Johnny Depp before he got totally weird. I watch him squirm. He looks toward Sheila Hurly, who's standing a few feet away chewing on a cuticle. She doesn't know what to do with herself, but she's dressed for the forest in tight jeans and sandals with rhinestones.

He looks at his shoes (cool blue-and-white Pumas), looks at Sheila, looks anywhere but at me.

Finally he blurts, "I know I'm supposed to be at Saint Mary's all the time, Ryan, but I can't. Charlotte just lays there. The whole thing creeps me out. I visited her. I did. A couple of times. Do you think she knows?"

"Probably not."

"Do you talk to her?"

"Sometimes."

"Well, next time tell her how I feel, okay, man? Be a good guy." He shuffles up to me so Sheila can't hear. "Tell her I still love her," he whispers, "and when she wakes up for her to call me."

"You're serious."

Now he looks hurt. "Totally. Say, 'I love you, and I want you back.' Except make sure she knows it's you talking for me and not for, you know, yourself."

"Don't worry about that."

He doesn't hear me. He's too busy being relieved. Now he can devote himself completely to Sheila. He grabs her hand, then her arm goes around his waist.

A hundred yards away, Betty's playing what passes for volleyball at the Flats. I watch her climb the air. Even in the fading light, it looks like her hair is on fire. I like thinking about her. Talking to somebody like Derek makes me have to reboot my entire mind.

That's when I see Andy and Kyle get up from the picnic table, the one with most of the food, of course, and head my way. Kyle's got hold of Andy's T-shirt like you would with a little kid who might wander off.

I'm wondering how this is going to go down. Andy and I have been avoiding each other.

"Ryan!" He says it like it's been years. When he gets close, I can see this big silly grin on his face. Bigger than usual. Sillier than usual. Definitely chemically induced. I look at Kyle, but he's no help.

"Everything okay, Andy?"

"Better than okay, man."

"Did you beat Derricotte and those guys?"

"I killed them."

Way down the hill somebody yells, "Look out," and when Andy turns away to look, I ask Kyle, "What's he on?"

"Something he took in the car. He had me drive."

"Are you gonna keep an eye on him?"

"Sure. If it's up to me, we're going home pretty soon, anyway. This isn't my scene."

Andy's big arm goes around my shoulder, and he pulls me into him. "We're still gonna be goons, aren't we?"

I pat his chest. "Absolutely."

"Want to practice? I just saw Teagarden down there. Let's find him and kick his ass."

I ask Kyle, "Did Chris try and start something?"

He shakes his head. "He's busy with Diane Kipnis."

"C'mon," says Andy, "let's get him."

"Let's eat first, okay? Carb up."

That gets Andy's attention. "What kind of carbs?"

"All kinds. An enormous variety of carbs. Kyle'll get you started. Right, Kyle? And I'll be right there."

Kyle points. "Teagarden was that way, so we'll go this way."

Andy's already on his way back to the food, but he bellows, "Awesome hat, Ryan. I'm gonna get me one just like it."

I watch Andy lose his balance and stumble. If Charlotte hadn't fallen off that horse, that'd be me, too.

I watch Betty sprint toward me up the hill. When she stops, I say, "You aren't even breathing hard."

"Volleyball." She points to a table about ten yards away. "Claire and Jason scored some food before Andy got hold of it."

I look for his yellow T-shirt, but it's starting to get dark. "I was such a jackass up here. One time some guy from Blair broke my nose."

"Why did you fight so much?"

"It started when Molly got so bad she couldn't sit up."

If that was too enigmatic, she didn't let on. The fact is I was like the fox that got caught in a trap and chewed at his leg to hurt the hurt. That's why I liked to fight. It didn't matter if I won or lost. I just wanted to hurt the hurt.

She leads me to the table: leftover pizza and bottled water. Claire guzzles an Evian without taking a breath and then says to Jason, "Scoot down, I want to put my head in your lap and look up at what's left of the clouds. I know all their names." She points. "Those big white ones are Accumulated, and the rest of them are all Nimble."

Claire has no more than disappeared from view when Betty says, "Now I suppose you'd like me to put my head in your lap and look at the clouds, too?"

A breeze comes up, and I grab for an empty paper bag so it won't blow away. I hear Andy laugh and then start coughing.

"Are you worried about him?" Betty asks.

I shake my head. "Kyle's with him. He'll be all right." I take a deep breath. "He was a pretty good friend in a lot of ways. But things kind of got out of hand."

From twenty yards away, I hear somebody say, "What happened to the music?"

Somebody else says, "Hold on. I'll get it."

Then nobody does, and I'm just turning around to see what the trouble is when a kid in hiking boots groans, "There's nothing here but Keith Urban. Who's Keith Urban?"

I lean forward, tilt my hat until it almost covers my eyes, and say to my friends: "We're coming to you live from Party Central, all set to go right into a commercial-free fifteen minutes of Keith Urban, rehab specialist and Nicole Kidman's main man. What's he got that I don't except killer cheekbones and the soul of a poet, right? But don't let's hold that against him. We'll start this set with something from the *Golden Road* album, 'You're Not Alone Tonight.' And don't forget, kids—dancing is allowed. Don't just lean on a tree when you can rock this place."

Betty laughs out loud as Claire sits up and says, "How cool was that?"

I add, "Let's send this one out to Charlotte."

Just then Derricotte climbs onto one of the picnic

tables, holds his bottle of beer up, and yells, "We own the night!"

"We usually split before that stuff starts," says Jason.

Betty says, "I wonder if somebody should point out that it's not quite dark yet, so it's premature to brag about owning the night."

Jason grins. "I'll go back and do that. I know he'll take it well. Derricotte's that kind of guy."

Walking to the Xterra, Betty says, "You know what, you guys. My car's at the hospital. Drop Ryan and me off there."

About half an hour later, we pull up in front of Betty's house. I look at the long lawn, the little porch, the lighted windows. It's dwarfed by the McMansions higher up on the block, but it feels more substantial. I can imagine this place being here when there was nothing else but a wide dirt road and orange groves.

"You still up for this?" Betty asks.

"Your grandparents don't know how I used to be, do they?"

She shakes her head. "Don't worry. They just like to meet my friends. Aren't your folks like that?"

"Your granddad's a cop, right? What am I going to talk to him about?"

Betty gets out of the car, so I do, too. We meet by the

right fender. She slips her arm through mine, and we start up the walk. "He reads. You know how to read. And if he asks you to prove it, don't move your lips."

There's a lawn mower right in the middle of the yard like somebody just gave up. On the front door is a big wreath. Really big.

"Grandma's crafty," Betty says. "In every sense of the word."

I look at the red berries and what are almost for sure silk flowers. "So she made this?"

"Oh, yeah. Esther doesn't believe in idle hands. I hope you aren't allergic to eucalyptus."

"It's huge."

"Esther thinks big."

"So your grandfather could shoot people, and your grandmother could make giant wreaths for their funerals."

She nods. "But let's just keep that between us for the time being." Then she opens the door and yells, "Anybody home?"

"In here!"

I follow her toward the living room. A stocky guy struggles to get out of his BarcaLounger, and a woman in purple pants puts down a magazine and stands up. There's a card table held in place by a half-finished game of solitaire. Stacks of paperback books. Lots of photographs— people in parkas and no parkas, long pants and short pants, boots and shoes and sandals. The same three people— Betty and her grandparents. Betty growing up, the other two getting older. But nobody who might be Betty's mother.

"This is my friend Ryan," Betty says. She tugs at me just a little. "And this is Maurice and Esther."

"Morrie," he says. "Nobody calls me Maurice."

"I call you Maurice," Esther insists.

"Nobody but her, then." He points to the couch. "Sit down, sit down. Maybe somebody on the distaff side of things could get us something to drink while I interrogate the suspect. Sorry. I mean chat with Ryan."

I'm on the couch by now, so it's easy for Betty to fuss with my hair, which is curly and has a mind of its own. "You'll be fine," she says on her way to the kitchen. "He doesn't bite."

Morrie settles back in his recliner. "It's true. I don't."

I can tell by the way he links his fingers across his stomach and stares up at the ceiling that I'm supposed to go first. I wonder how many times he's done this. Is it fun for him, a relief from cards and fiction and TV?

I venture, "Betty says you like to read."

He nods. "I do. I think television is stupid. I've got one in the other room, but I don't watch it much. Just *Law and Order* and wrestling sometimes."

"Do you like mysteries and stuff like that?"

Another nod. "Absolutely. Do you know who's the best hands-down crime writer there is? Dostoyevsky. The Russian. Do you know *Crime and Punishment*?"

I nod. "A little, actually. Somebody kills a pawnbroker, right?"

"Exactly. He thinks he can take her money, do good with it, and everything will be hunky-dory." Morrie shakes his head. "Doesn't work that way." Finally he looks at me. "What are you reading?"

"Right now just stuff for school."

"Like?"

Actually I've been studying more lately, but Betty's grandfather either makes me nervous or I know I'm supposed to be nervous. "If I can't remember, are you going to tie me to a chair?"

He laughs and shouts so they can hear him in the kitchen, "He's all right!"

"Leave him alone, Maurice," Esther says.

"I'm telling you, he's all right." Morrie looks at me. "You're all right, aren't you, Ryan?"

"Yes, sir."

He lurches forward and scoots until he can put his feet on the floor. "Do you know the Joe Wambaugh novel called *The New Centurions*?"

I shake my head.

"Old cop played by George C. Scott in the movie and

a young cop. I forget who that was. The point is I'm the old cop. I don't run in anywhere with my gun out. I leave that to the cowboys. I know people. I've got a couple of snitches. I get the job done that way. Almost thirty years on the job, and I've never fired a shot at anybody."

He reminds me of another old guy from the gym, a guy I've seen in the steam room a couple of times. He's got a jagged scar down the middle of his chest from an operation, probably some big-time bypass. I just can't see Morrie's scars. The ones inflicted by Betty's mother—the junkie and thief.

He grins this time. "I like your hat," he says. "That's classy. Is that the new style? I hope to god it is. I'm sure tired of seeing kids with their pants down to their knees and their caps on backward."

I turn the hat around in my hands. "I just . . . I don't know. I was at the hospital the other day, and there was this old black-and-white movie on with a bunch of guys in cool hats, so I bought one."

"You're at the hospital for that Silano girl, too?" He shakes his head. "That was a damn shame. Is that how you know Betty?"

"Kind of."

Betty and Esther come back in with stuff on a tray. The pitcher is tall and clear, but the glasses have black-and-white stripes, the kind convicts always wear in cartoons.

Esther hands me a full glass, and I give that to Betty, who's now sitting beside me on the couch.

"Kool-Aid," Betty says. "We got out the good stuff just for you."

"I'm flattered."

"Morrie has a gun," Betty says. "If you aren't nice to me, he'll shoot you, won't you, Granddad?"

Morrie nods. "Right where it'll do the most good."

Esther pretends to be stern. "Stop teasing Ryan. If you want to talk about guns, tell him about Alaska."

"Grandma, I was five."

"Oh, you remember."

"What I remember," Betty says, "is Granddad telling this story."

"Well, then, you tell it, Maurice."

He sighs and squirms a little and generally acts like he's just been asked to paint the house. But I'm happy to settle in. His voice hums like an air conditioner.

"Well," he says, "we're on this trip to Alaska, okay? A guy on the force has this motor home, and he rents it to any cop who wants it for a couple of weeks. So I make the arrangements and off we go. We're not looking for Betty's dad, who's up there somewhere with a bunch of other misfits—"

Esther warns him, "Maurice."

"I'm saying we're not doing that. I'm saying we're

up there driving around and looking at one moose after another. And we're in Seward with a week's worth of dirty clothes, so we go into this Laundromat down by the river where they process salmon."

Esther says, "I learned about Alaska and what the people are like by going to the Laundromats."

Morrie nods. "This one was a pip, I have to say. The smaller the town, the more likely it is that there'll be a shower for people who come in from the honest-to-God wilderness and haven't changed their clothes for six months."

"So we go into this one," Esther says, "and there's guns on the dryers so people will know they're taken, and people not walking around half naked or anything but with towels or the worst-looking bathrobes I've ever seen, and they've all got beards and long hair—"

"And those are the women," Morrie says right on cue.

"But Betty, who's five, wins their hearts."

"I still have a weakness for hairy men in towels," Betty says.

"Pretty soon," Esther says, "we know everybody's name and most of their life stories. Somebody went next door for beer, and we just stayed there for hours." She points toward a desk in the corner. "I've got their addresses somewhere, some of them, anyway. They were none of them fixed. Either in care of somebody or general delivery."

"It's legal to carry sidearms in Alaska," Morrie says. "And there's a lot less gun-related crime than down here."

Betty stands up, goes across the room, and kisses her grandfather before she says, "Time to take Ryan home. Then I'll be right back."

"It's not even nine o'clock," says Esther.

"Ryan goes to bed early. He wants to be healthy, wealthy, and wise."

Once we get in the car, I put on my seat belt and tell Betty, "They're nice."

"They liked you. Morrie knows who your mom is. She sang for some benefit he was part of. When the library flooded, I think."

"We used to be like you guys are. I mean just glad to be home and reading a book or watching something on TV. Then Molly died and . . . I don't know. I just kind of went to my own version of Deadville."

"Well, you're back now."

I nod. "So far, so good."

I give Betty a few directions, and pretty soon we pull up in front of my house.

"Wow," she says. "It's nice."

I open my door a little. "Listen."

The music drifts out an open window. I tell Betty, "It's my mom and her friends. She's the soprano."

Betty fiddles with her keys. "My god," she says. "Did you plan this?"

"I'm not that resourceful."

We make out for a long time, then stop and listen to the music—Verdi, I think. We handle each other modestly and carefully and get only slightly disoriented and disordered until one of us pauses. Betty has a bottle of water in her purse, and we take turns sipping from that. Neither one of us "tries anything." Finally she kisses me in a different way. I get out of the car, and she drives away.

I watch the taillights of Betty's hybrid until they disappear, then walk into the house. Mom and four of her friends are still practicing, so I lean on the wall and listen. Mr. Vega—who seems to have more than thirty-two teeth and is showing them all—stands by my mother. I catch her eye and point upstairs, meaning, "I'm going to bed." She nods and blows me a kiss. I'm in such a good mood that if my dad were here, I'd eat mung beans with him.

When I get to my room, the first thing I do is dial Betty's number. I do it fast because I know I'm supposed to do this or something like it. It's the weird resentment of the hungry man being forced to eat. I want to call her, but

I don't want to have to call her. When she picks up, I say, "It's me. I just wanted to make sure you got home okay."

"I had to dodge a couple of mammoths, but I'm used to that. Are they still singing?"

"They're about done, I think."

I sit on the bed and then lie down. On the wall behind my computer, I've got a map of the solar system. On Mercury, Andy's favorite planet, he'd weigh about seventy-two pounds.

"You'll never guess who asked me out the other day. Jay Farber."

I'm still looking at my map. On Mercury, Jay would weigh about nine pounds. I tell her, "You should absolutely go. You'll like Mrs. Farber."

"What's Mrs. Farber have to do with it?"

"She drives Jay everywhere. They're inseparable. They'll probably both kiss you good night."

"You're a pretty cool customer for somebody who carries an extra pair of pants in a bag."

"Hey, those are vintage slacks from Aardvark's. Wait until you see Jay Farber in those plaid cargo pants his mother buys him."

"I'm not going anywhere with Jay Farber. But you were jealous for a minute."

"I absolutely was."

"You know, Ryan. Now that you've seen my alabaster

skin in the moonlight, there are a few things you have to do: Meet me before first period, walk me to every class, and text me all day. Sit with me at lunch, and take me to Paris for the weekend."

"So," I ask, reading from *The Boyfriend's Guide to Harmony,* "where should I meet you in the morning?"

NINE

A few weeks later, we're on our way to the hospital. Betty looks cute (white blouse tied right at her belly button, some kind of webby-looking sandals), and I've got on those linen pants from Aardvark's and a cool new belt. I like thinking about what to wear. The other day I laid out some clothes on my bed, then switched things around—this shirt with those cords, that sweater with those jeans. I would never tell anybody I did that. And when I put things away, I looked at myself in the mirror and asked the same question Betty asked a few weeks ago: Who are you, anyway? I like my new life, I guess, but it all seems slightly prefabricated. Something I've just moved into. A tract house like a lot of others.

"Let's stop at Starbucks," Betty says. "I need to get a job application, anyway, because my granddad will match me dollar for dollar if I put the money away for college. But mostly I just need something with the word *grande* in it. I've been half asleep all day."

Even from a couple hundred yards away, I can see a lot of people sitting outside playing cards and drinking coffee. We score a parking place almost right in front. When we get out, Betty loops her arm through mine.

"Hey, you guys!"

It's Elton and Leigh Ann. We make our way over to the table.

Leigh Ann pulls out one of the empty chairs. She looks concentrated. Cute, but compact. Her T-shirt says TRIUMPH, and her hair is motorcycle-tire black.

"What I want to do is lie down," Betty says. "But I'll settle for this." She puts her purse and sweater on the table. "Keep an eye on these, okay? We'll be right back."

When we're barely inside, she asks, "Are you okay with this? Give me fifteen minutes and I'll be fine."

"Charlotte's not going anywhere."

Betty massages my arm the way the witch in "Hansel and Gretel" might—to see how tasty I am. "I think you're a little stronger," she says. "Do you think you're a little stronger?"

"I don't know. It's not like I've been working out

for months." I feel her lean into me. "Are you all right?" I ask.

"I'm not sick or anything. It's just three weeks till the end of school, and I've got all this work to do."

"You're getting all A's."

"So far, but it's easy to slide down to a B. And you don't get scholarships with B's."

"You're not going to get any B's. I'm getting B's and glad of it."

"I'm just going to put my chin on your shoulder and doze off."

I glance outdoors and ask, "What's the story on Leigh Ann?"

Betty mumbles, "Vegan. Black belt in tae kwon do. Shows up at school with some of the weirdest zines I've ever seen."

"Well, this sounds like fun."

Outside we sit down and wait for Elton and Leigh Ann to finish the card game they're playing. It's nice in the sun. I like the way these linen pants feel. My mind's calendar rolls back. I'm so different from the way I was. I'm either fine or I'm pretending to be fine, and I'm not sure I'd know the difference if somebody pointed it out. Betty drinks her coffee fast, fanning it with her hand to make it cool.

Just then two little girls walk past. They're in their

school uniforms—a kind of checkered jumper—but I recognize Jason's sister, Jo Ann.

All of a sudden she stops, looks over at us, and points. When she whispers to her friend, she does that thing where she puts her hand up to the other girl's ear. Which just kills me. Molly used to do that.

"Where'd you go?" asks Betty.

"What? I didn't go anywhere."

"Yeah, you did."

"No, I didn't." If I lie to her, does that mean she lies to me?

I wave at Jo Ann. In no time flat, both girls are standing in front of me.

I ask, "What are you guys up to?"

Jo Ann says, "This is my friend Penny. She's praying for Charlotte, too. Without ceasing."

"Except on Tuesdays and Thursdays," Penny says, "when I have violin."

Betty says, "Good for you guys."

"We have to go to church now," Jo Ann says. Then they turn in unison and walk away.

Elton picks up the deck of cards and shuffles them. He cuts the deck and shows me the six of diamonds. "Is this your card?" he asks, and then grins.

Leigh Ann asks, "Are you on your way to see Charlotte?"

"After this, yeah."

"She the same?"

"Pretty much."

She says to me, "You are so much better for her than Derek. You're nice, you show up on time, and you're not going to fool around with some other girl in a coma."

"Ryan's not Charlotte's boyfriend," says Betty. "He's just a friend."

Leigh Ann looks at Betty over the top of her glasses. "That's what I said, Bennett: *better* than a boyfriend."

Betty just stares into space. I'm thinking about something my mother told me about reincarnation. How the soul more or less rests for a while and absorbs what it's been through before it comes back again. So where is Charlotte's soul, and what's it up to?

Leigh Ann prods Elton. "Tell them what you told me," she says. "About after graduation."

Leigh Ann is starting to remind me of one of those fish with spines, the kind you touch and your finger swells up.

Elton inhales before he starts. "I just said that I'm probably going to enlist."

That makes even Betty sit up. "In the army?" she asks.

Elton nods. "I give 'em four years; they pay for college."

I remind him, "You could get shot, man."

He shakes his head. "They'll make me a cook."

"I think it's cool," says Leigh Ann.

Elton nudges Betty. "You get it, don't you, Bennett? I mean, you're going to be a cop."

She answers without opening her eyes. "I said I might."

Leigh Ann points a wooden coffee stirrer at me. "What about you?"

"What about me?"

"Oh, I forgot. You have a career holding Charlotte Silano's hand."

I tell her, "I'm sixteen. Call me in two years, okay?"

Betty asks, "Can we talk about something else? This isn't helping my headache."

Somebody walking by coughs, then flicks a cigarette into the street.

Leigh Ann frowns at his back, then says, "Tell Charlotte to make up her mind, Ryan. Right now she's between the memorial page and the regular page. I'm on the yearbook staff, and we're not going to start a whole new limbo section just for her."

"You don't know anything about Charlotte," I say.

"We've got a pool," she says. "Everybody puts in a buck and picks a date. Closest one wins."

I look right at her. "That's just stupid."

Betty's reaching for her purse and her sweater when Chris Teagarden rumbles by in his Mustang. He leans across the kid riding shotgun and yells, "Ryan!" Then he gives me the finger.

"What was that about?" asks Elton once the light has changed and Chris is half a block away.

"He and I got into it once at a soccer game."

"You know," Leigh Ann says, "Charlotte shouldn't have eaten so much meat all her life. That stuff comes back to haunt you."

I push away from the table, and my chair falls over. Betty and I walk to her car. People bustle in and out of the bank next to the Starbucks or use the ATM.

"Well," I say, "that got weird."

"You drive, okay?" Betty says. "I'm about two centimeters away from a migraine."

I don't say anything; Betty doesn't say anything. At the corner of Arroyo and Glenarm, there's some new graffiti. Huge block letters—SOON—across the usual outline of the mammoth.

I point to it. "That stupid thing."

"Like Leigh Ann's stupid?"

"I didn't say Leigh Ann was stupid. I said that pool is stupid. Who gambles on when somebody's going to die?"

"It's not like we've got a thousand friends, Ryan. You could've let it go. She's pretending to be a hard-boiled journalist, that's all."

I say, "Since when are they our friends, and since when are you going to be a cop?"

"I told Elton that when we were going out. His grandfather was in the service and so was his dad. Just like my grandfather is third-generation law enforcement. So he says he's going to sign up, and I say, 'Yeah, I might be a cop.' Talking about that was a lot better than listening to him play the guitar." Betty fumbles in her purse. "God, I wish I could find some Motrin."

I pull over and put the car in Park. "I'm going to walk the rest of the way. Rhett says it'll be good for me."

She puts her hand up to shield her eyes. "It's just three blocks."

I grab my gym bag as I get out of the car. "Better than nothing."

She reaches for me. I pull away but lean back in as she eases herself into the driver's seat and asks, "How long are we going to keep this up?"

"Keep what up?"

"Going to the hospital."

"I don't know."

"We never do anything. We talk on the phone and watch Charlotte breathe."

"I started this, Betty, and I'm going to finish it. I just can't stand the idea that she's in that room all by herself."

"Except she's not all by herself. Her parents are there; physical therapists are there; nurses are there."

I take a step back. "Then don't go."

She just reaches for her sunglasses, puts the car in Drive, and eases away. "Don't worry. I won't."

I yell after her, "And I'm not joining the army, either. That's really stupid!"

I'm my usual bifurcated self: pompous and ashamed. It was a dumb argument that I could've sidestepped at any time. But I'm right. Or at least more right than she is.

She hasn't been gone ten seconds when my cell phone rings. It's Andy.

"Where are you, man?" he asks.

"Almost to the hospital."

"Well, get your ass over here. Kyle and I are in the tree house, and this is either some serious creeper bud we're smoking or there are fourteen dwarfs down there."

I remember the tree house and the light through the leaves. I remember sitting there with the volume on my iPod turned all the way up.

"Don't smoke it all," I tell him. "I'm on my way."

I trudge the three blocks from the bus stop to Andy's house. Through the front window I can see the huge TV and Andy's brothers chasing each other. I walk around the side like I used to, past Andy's car and then the old truck his father drives, all the way to the back. If anything, there are more garden gnomes, and all of them eerily facing the same way. I hear Andy telling Kyle, "Yeah, there's Pervo and Stupid and Droopy . . ." And then he's laughing too hard to go on.

I sit down between a couple of dwarfs. The mind-crow glides by Saint Mary's, where Monica and Dr. Silano are talking; past Betty's house, where she's trying to call me; past my house, where my mom is sipping red wine and looking at a cookbook. Then he comes back and lands on the nearest statue. I like his bright eyes and glossy feathers. I like it that he isn't some chubby pigeon with a note tied to his skinny leg. But his message is clear: Live in this world. *This* one.

"Hey, Ryan? Is that you down there? What are you doing? Get up here!"

I look up at Andy's round face. He's got chocolate smeared all around his mouth, so he looks like the biggest four-year-old in the world.

"Let me borrow your car first."

Kyle bellows, "Beer run! And get chips."

I get to my feet and hold out both hands. "Just throw the keys down. I'll be right back."

I am super-careful. Signaling to change lanes, stopping at every stop sign, yielding to anybody and everybody. So when I get to Chris Teagarden's house, I'm solid in the world.

He's outside in his LBJ gym shorts, T-shirt, and flip-flops like any kid doing what his father told him. The hard stream of the hose he's holding is driving some blue-gray blobs of something toward the gutter, so they can eventually make a manatee sick.

I cross the brown lawn, coming at him from an angle. He doesn't look up; he just says, "Hey, Ryan."

I tell him, "I'm the guy who trashed your car a couple of months ago."

He's got a new look—spiky, bleached-out hair like that old rocker Billy Idol. He says, "I figured it was you and Andy. I've just been busy beating up fourth-graders and taking their lunch money."

"So I'll pay for, you know, whatever it cost."

"Fifteen hundred. My dad was really pissed. He wanted to sue."

I shrug. What am I going to do, argue with him? I'll be mowing lawns till I'm fifty.

"All at once, too, Glazier. No payments."

The front of his house is almost hidden by ferns. There are big rocks among those, rocks that had to be trucked in. "Did you used to play back there when you were little?"

He half turns around. "Yeah. We'd hold off the radioactive aliens from behind those boulders."

I'm closer to him now, off the so-called lawn and onto the sloping, cracked driveway. I'm pretty sure his arms are bigger, the biceps, anyway. He's the kind of guy who'd start going to a gym. We're that close to being friends.

"I'll get the money somehow."

He pivots to face me, then pulls the big trigger on the nozzle so that I have to jump back to keep from getting my shoes wet.

"Couldn't resist, could you, Chris?"

"I'm bad to the bone."

"You wish."

I'm halfway to the car when he yells, "Two hundred."

So I turn around. "You just said—"

"I lied. You're not that good a shot."

Driving back, I follow the mind-crow, who is the sky's favorite. We wind down streets named after priests or missions, go past the last orange trees out of the hundreds that used to be here.

When we get to town, the streetlights have just started to hand out the small change in their deep pockets. I know my mother is cooking jasmine rice. I know Betty is worried because we argued. I know Charlotte is maybe/maybe not.

When I get to Andy's, I pull the car into his driveway and sit. His father's truck is gone and the house is dark, so

Andy's cranked up his old boom box. "We Are the Champions" almost makes the leaves of the trees flutter. Freddie Mercury in his black-and-white leotard purrs, "I've paid my dues . . ."

I just can't walk along the side of the house again, grab hold of those rungs, and climb. Out here things are and they aren't. They're fading and coming into focus. At seven thirty-two on a Wednesday afternoon, it's not quite light, not quite dark.

So I put the keys under the seat and catch the next bus.

TEN

A couple of days later, I hold the door of Weight World for Miranda Corin, an eleventh-grader. She swings her blue gym bag aside so it won't catch in the door, then looks up at the sky, closes her eyes, and opens her mouth like the sun is dispensing vitamins. Her lip gloss or lipstick is white or whitish. That and her razzle-dazzle outfit (star-spangled tights and an all-bite-no-bark top) makes me feel like I'm in someone's presence compared to just standing beside her.

"I liked jogging with you," she says. "Do you always come at this time?"

"It depends."

"Well, I'm always here at eleven. Maybe we'll bump into each other." Then she leans forward and kisses the air right next to my cheek.

I'm pretty sure that this is Miranda's way. I mean, I know it is. I've seen her flit through the halls of LBJ High for a couple of years. But she never landed anywhere close to me until today.

So I'm flattered and baffled. Not that I'd do anything just for a ride in Miranda's Lexus, but I don't even know how to break up with somebody. I spent two years in a kind of coma while everybody else was learning the ropes: liking and being liked, leaving and being left.

And I can just hear myself asking Miranda to swing by the hospital on our way to Happyland so I can hold Charlotte Silano's hand.

I'm brooding about all this on my way to the bus stop, but then I look up. A giant crane is lowering a great big sign onto the top of the old McAllister building: MAMMOTH SAVINGS AT FAIRWAY BANK. The next thing is a mammoth galloping toward me: orange fur, plastic tusks, gross-looking trunk, and high-tops.

It holds out a piece of paper. "Open a checking account today and get a free toaster."

"You're kidding." Automatically I take the application.

"No way. I've seen 'em. They're cool. Silver or white to, like, match your decor or whatever."

"I meant you're kidding about the whole mammoth thing. It was an ad campaign?"

The mammoth nods and straightens its head. "Is that you, Glazier?"

"Yeah, who are you?"

"Benson. Greg Benson. Your dad and my dad work together. Wait a minute. Hold this paperwork, okay?"

So I do while he struggles with his head. Once it's off and tucked under his arm, I recognize him. His hair is matted and stuck to his scalp. He's dripping wet.

"Makes you want to go to college, doesn't it?" he says.

"I thought you went to Berkeley."

"For like twenty minutes. Way too intense for me up there. Too easy to party, too. I go to, like, three meetings a day to stay out of trouble." He points up. "A power greater than myself, right?"

"Right."

"You okay? You were kind of an all-star for a while."

"Not lately."

"I'm back living with my parents. I tried, you know, on my own, but that didn't work." He looks at the bag in my right hand. "My sponsor wants me to join a gym. Are you playing soccer again?"

"A little."

"You should. You were good."

I can't help but ask, "Did you know all along this whole mammoth thing was bogus?"

He shakes his head. The real one. "I'm just making seven bucks an hour. Wear this outfit through Saturday and then next week clean up the graffiti, which is basically water-based paint, anyway, so that's no big deal."

"Cynthia Wixen thought the world was coming to an end."

He shrugs. "So now she gets a toaster instead." He puts the big, furry head back on and holds out one hand. "See you, man. I gotta get back to work."

At the hospital I stop at the nurses' station and tell Monica, "That mammoth thing turns out to be some lame ad campaign."

Monica has three charts open at once. "What mammoth thing?" she asks absently.

"Nothing. Forget it. Charlotte okay?"

"Uh-huh."

But I don't get all the way to Charlotte because Betty is standing in the doorway of Thad's room. She looks great in Quiksilver shorts and a T-shirt from the Humane Society featuring a shower of cats and dogs. And Thad's standing, too. No IV, either.

Betty holds out one arm, and I walk up to her close enough so she can put it around my waist. I feel slightly guilty for even thinking about Miranda Corin.

"And now," Betty says, "guess who's better. Here's a

hint—he's handsome, he's the mayor of Deadville, and, girls, he's single!"

I tell Thad, "You do look pretty good."

"New drug. I've been good for forty-eight hours." He crosses his fingers. "I'm even hungry. Another two thousand tests and ten pounds, and I'm out of here."

I ask Betty, "Did you see the sign for mammoth savings?"

She nods. "On my way over."

I put my lips right up to her ear. "It's very cool that you come here. I know it's not much fun, and there really are nine thousand other things we could be doing."

She takes my face between her hands. "What's got into you?"

I point. "I'm just going to, you know, check in next door, and then we'll get out of here."

When I'm sure I'm by myself, I walk right up to Charlotte and, for the first time ever, hold her hand. I put it between both of mine. I say to her (or maybe *implore* is a better verb), "Please come back. Please. I can't keep doing this. Okay? You know you're going to be fine. So do it. Nobody likes a tease."

That's when she starts to sweat. Just like that, her face is shiny and damp. One big drop rolls from her hairline, down and around her eye, before it slants toward one ear.

I yell for Betty, who takes a look and dashes down the

hall. I hit the call button. Thad must have seen Betty smoke by, so he yells, "What's wrong, man?" But I don't answer. Automatically I go to the other wall and stand there. I don't want to be in the way.

An intern shows up, then another doctor. They hover over Charlotte. Somebody throws back the sheet and checks out her legs. Then I hear the initials *OR* and the word *clots* and the sound of a gurney turning a corner at top speed and bumping into the jamb. One of her monitors goes haywire as she's lifted off the bed and onto the gurney, the intern handles two of the IVs, and they're gone. The room is so empty. Betty's holding my hand so tight it hurts. "You think we should call Jill?" she asks.

"Maybe we better."

We're in the waiting room and we have been for a while. Betty pretends to read a magazine, then hands it to me, and I pretend. Or we take turns walking down to the window at the end of the hall. I know I didn't bring this crisis on, but the coincidence is pretty disorienting.

All of a sudden, Jill walks in with Derek.

"How's she doing?" Jill asks.

I tell her, "Nobody knows."

Derek checks his million-dollar phone. "Then what am I doing here?" he asks.

Jill punches him in the arm. "Charlotte's sicker, okay? And if something happens, you've only seen her once."

Derek takes off his sunglasses and waves them at her. "You should talk. The only time you showed up, you were so stoned, you could hardly get in the elevator."

I slam a magazine down. "Shut up, both of you!"

Jill tells me, "You shut up. You think you're better than us. I bought dope from you and Andy."

"Not from me you didn't."

Betty steps up beside me. "Act like you're in a hospital, you guys."

"I'm the one who's Charlotte's best friend," Jill says. "Who are you? You're just a babysitter."

I reach for Betty's arm. "C'mon, let's take a little walk."

We're almost to the window at the end of the hall when she says, "She could be getting worse. In the movies when they wake up, they just wake up."

A nurse comes around the corner. There's nobody else in the hall, but she herds us toward the fire extinguisher, anyway, before she says, "The ultrasound showed a blood clot. That's why she was sweating so much."

I tell her, "I was talking to her right before this happened."

"Are you thinking you had something to do with this? People who are immobile throw blood clots all the time.

The OR team just did a standard procedure. Charlotte's in recovery. Her mother's with her. She should be fine, but Dr. Silano doesn't want visitors anymore."

"Ever?" I ask.

The nurse shrugs. "At least until he says so."

ELEVEN

A couple of weeks later, I'm on my way out of the house when Dad pulls up. He's home early. I watch him get out of the car. He's moving pretty slow.

I walk toward him. "You okay?"

"You drive," he says, handing me the keys.

"Where?"

"To the gym."

"You need your stuff."

He points. "It's in the trunk."

I've never driven my dad's car. The big leather seat is like a throne. I find the buttons that make the seat glide and angle the mirrors. When I turn the key, I barely hear the engine.

As I ease away from the curb, Dad asks, "Who taught you to drive, anyway?"

"Mom did. Then I took drivers' ed last semester and got my license."

"Did you tell me?"

"Probably not."

"I couldn't wait to get my driver's license."

"Why?" I keep my eyes on the road.

"There was this girl I wanted to ask out."

He's looking a little better but not much. He'll either tell me what's going on or he won't. No way am I begging him.

I ask, "City streets okay, or should I take the freeway?"

"What?"

I glance over at him. He is so thin. "What's up with the vegan thing, anyway? Are you supposed to lose that much weight?"

"I know, I know. Dr. Williams told me to take better care of myself."

I've got my iPod in my gym bag, but I can't imagine which of the songs would be appropriate for this ride.

"What's the news about Charlotte Silano, Ryan? Is she better? Worse? The same?"

What's the news about Charlotte Silano, Ryan? Each word is like a box he has to lift and line up with the one before.

I tell him, "Pretty much the same. I don't go to the hospital anymore. Her dad doesn't want her to have visitors."

"That doesn't sound good."

I look over at him. "Are you sure you want to do this?"

He nods. "I think it'll help. I think I need to get out of the lab. You just drive. I'll be fine."

At Weight World I park as far away from everybody else as I can. My father has this car washed twice a week and detailed every six months. I'm not going to be the one who parks by some beater and gets a ding in it.

"Get the trunk for me," he says.

I can't see a place for the key. "How?"

He grabs the ring and presses an "Open Sesame" button.

I watch him take out a bright red gym bag with white handles. I look at it, then him, then it.

"Your mother bought it."

"No kidding."

He unzips it and looks inside. Everything is folded or rolled or tucked. He did that. It's absolutely his way. He's always switching laundries because his shirts aren't perfect.

Inside we wait at the desk while Mitzi tells somebody, "She talks to Raoul again and I am all up in her face!" Then she folds up her phone and says, "Hi, Ryan." She points to the big speaker hanging from the nearest exposed beam. We usually play Name That Tune.

I've already listened, but I pretend to listen harder.

"Wu-Tang Clan. But I'm not sure what track."

"Half a point off but still good." She's got a big smile for my dad. "Now here's a guy who needs a protein shake."

"It's his first time." I make the introductions.

Out comes one hand with long, silver, intergalactic nails. "Your son is awesome."

While Dad fills out a little paperwork, I scope the place out. I know some of the people now, at least enough to say hi to. I'm starting to want a pair of gloves with the finger parts cut off. Not that I'm getting such massive calluses from the tremendous amounts of weight I've been lifting. I just think they look cool.

I ask Mitzi, "Is Rhett here?"

She shakes her head. She always wears a silver hat with a bill, and her ponytail comes out the back through that little igloo-entrance hole just above the adjustable straps. "Not yet," she says.

"You know what? I can get my dad started. I know the drill."

"Would you, Ryan? We're short-handed, so that would be great."

I point him toward the locker room, then dig out my cell, sit down on the nearest bench, and call Betty.

"Where are you?" she asks.

"The gym with my dad. Something happened at work. He's kind of a wreck."

"I called the hospital. Charlotte's the same."

A woman goes by in an outfit made for a smaller person. I watch a guy rip the rubber band off his ponytail, shake his hair loose, and pick up a set of heavier dumbbells. Charlotte is still adrift.

Betty says, "I dreamed about her last night. It was just a regular dream. We were at school playing volleyball. She was ordering everybody around like she used to. Listen, good luck with your dad. Call me when you get home."

Ten minutes later I watch my father plod toward me. Mom has bought him a bright red warm-up outfit, so he looks like somebody who's on fire and doesn't care.

I get him on the treadmill, go over a couple of easy programs, show him how to straddle the belt until it gets moving, and hit the Start button. Then I climb on mine. Together but separate.

"In what way are you awesome?" he asks.

I look at him.

"That girl with the talons said you were awesome."

"Oh, that. She likes music, too. What'd you think?"

"I didn't know."

"And they aren't talons. They're just plastic. They come off."

He mutters, "She looks like everything's plastic." Then

he points to the control panel. "Okay, I haven't run in a while, but this isn't difficult at all."

"Dad, we're crawling. You want to pick up the pace, hit the little arrow pointing up and then three."

I watch him do it, then I angle up higher and hit five.

"Can I use my hands?" he asks.

"To keep your balance? Sure. Just grab the safety rails."

He starts to breathe through his mouth as a big guy in thrashed gym trunks over some blue Lycra bicycle pants walks between us and stares out the window toward Myrtle Avenue. He's breathing hard and massaging those big muscles on his shoulders (trapezius, for the record). He's worked on those so long, they look like what's left of a huge pair of wings.

When he turns around, he exhales with a *whoosh* and nods at me. "Hey, man."

"Yeah."

When he's gone, Dad asks, "Who's he?"

"Just some gym rat. He's okay."

"It's like code, isn't it? All that 'Hey, man'–'Yeah' stuff."

"Sort of, I guess."

"Why didn't he say anything to me?" my father asks.

"He doesn't know you."

"You're saying he knows you?"

"I show up."

My dad thinks this over before he says, "Point taken."

We jog a little. I start to sweat, and it feels good.

"How long do we do this?" Dad asks.

"We can stop whenever."

"How about now. Let's lift some weights."

He hits the Stop button and lets the momentum carry him off the back of the machine so that he's behind me when he says, "At work today this guy lost his daughter. She was camping with some church group, got all turned around, fell off a cliff, and now she's dead. He came in, but we sent him home."

I don't turn around yet. "You went to work the day after Molly died."

"That was different. It made me concentrate."

"If you say so." I step off the machine.

He leans over and kneads his thigh muscles, which are powerful-looking. "After Molly's funeral," he says, "I couldn't sleep on my right side. It was like I'd been beat up."

"Well, my legs hurt all the time." I lead the way to the nearest machine and fiddle with the weight.

"Did you tell your mother?" he asks.

"That my legs hurt? No, she would've worried. I told Andy. He said for me to shut up, look at the screen, and kill some more aliens."

"Probably good advice. I wish he'd told me what to do."

I point. "Do you want to use free weights or a machine?"

"What's the difference?"

"Pussies use the machines."

"Up to you."

I shove him. A little. "Sit on the bench. Put your arms here, reach down and grab the bar with both hands, and bring it up. This'll give you big guns."

"What are those?"

"Eighteen-inch biceps."

"What are mine now?"

"You don't want to know."

He does a few repetitions. "This isn't so hard."

I lean down and show him the stack of weight bars. "Try twenty."

He does and I watch him plant his feet. Which I kick. "Don't cheat. Just use your arms."

"Do you do anything but give advice?"

"I'm just saying what Rhett would say."

A minute later he watches me wipe down the chrome and plastic. "I'm not toxic, Ryan. I'm your father."

"It's what you're supposed to do."

I'm on my sixth or seventh rep when he says, "It was

like I never slept. I know I did, but that's not what I remember. What I remember is being awake and thinking about her under the ground."

"Well, I played music so loud, I think I hurt my hearing. For a while I thought I couldn't swallow. I drank malts and smoothies and things I could pour down me."

"I'd just lie there by your mother. I couldn't touch her."

We don't look at each other, but we keep talking. We could be a couple of spies exchanging vital information in a B movie.

I point. "Wipe that machine down, and do another set of ten if you can."

"I'm not dizzy or anything."

"I didn't say you were."

He straddles the marble-colored seat. "I started losing weight," he says, "because this guy at the lab—Smart guy, too. Can rattle off pi as long as you can stand to listen— told me about this study where rats who ate less lived longer."

"Vegan rats?"

"No, I thought I'd just combine the two modalities."

"Why'd you want to live longer? You just said you were miserable. You couldn't sleep and everything hurt."

"I didn't say it made sense. I tried running more, but my knees went. Cooking gave me something else to do."

"Something besides thinking about Molly?"

"Exactly."

I lead him to the lat pull-down machine. I sit and show him. I go slow and touch the long bar to my chest. He tries and I have to help him keep things even. It's like he's totally unbalanced.

"Don't overcompensate!"

He says, "I'm not. It feels the same on both sides."

"Well, it's not the same. Put your hands closer together."

"Can I stop for a minute?"

"Let go; I've got it."

He pretends his sneaks need tying. Then fusses with his socks. Everything's brand-new.

I tell him, "I thought you were nuts. Mom and I'd come home from the hospital, and there you'd be eating two ounces of seaweed."

He reaches up again, and I pull the bar down to him. "I was a little nuts," he says. "I can fix anything, Ryan. At the lab I'm the go-to guy. I'm a legend. But I couldn't fix what was happening at the hospital."

"So you drove into L.A. to buy mung beans?"

He takes a couple of deep breaths. "I'd get off work and go by the hospital. Your mother had been there all day, and all I could stand was ten minutes because I knew Molly was going to die. I knew it, Ryan. I know people who know people. I talked to oncologists in Europe. The kind of tumor Molly had, by the time there were any symptoms at all, it was too late. I told your mother this, and she wouldn't believe me. She wanted to try everything, and you know what that did, don't you? Made Molly suffer more. Did you see her in that mask she had to wear for radiation? My god. All those awful treatments for nothing. I'd get up in the middle of the night and talk to Molly. I'd tell her I loved her and wanted her to go." He looks up at the bar. "Why can't I keep this thing level?"

I steady the bar for him. "Why didn't you tell me this then? I thought you were a callous bastard."

He doesn't look at me. He could be talking to the machine when he says, "You were in no shape to listen to much of anything, especially the kind of bad news I had."

So there's my dad knowing that and my mom denying it and me as high as I could get without falling down. I grope for the bench and sit beside my father. He's facing one way, and I'm facing the other. I feel him lean into me.

"Are you all right?" he asks.

"I should probably get a drink of water."

"I'll go with you."

Somebody passes us with new silver shoes, like a messenger of the gods. My dad drapes a towel over my shoulders and says, "I'm proud of you for sticking with this. It paid off. You look different. I can see it. How long would it take me to be different?"

I press the little handle and nudge him to go first. "A couple of months, at least, but you have to eat more."

He drinks for a long time, nods, and says, "And show up three times a week." Then drinks some more.

"If you can, yeah."

"We'd come together or meet here."

"If you want, sure."

As we walk away, he gets hold of my T-shirt and tugs, not pulling me toward him or anything, just straightening it. "I might want to go to Athens," he says. "There's this thing there called the Tower of the Winds."

"Which is what?" I ask.

"People used to think it was a clock—water on the inside, sun on the outside—but it might be related to the Antikythera Mechanism. Nobody really knows what that is, but now people are thinking the two of them might be related. A little anyhow. I just thought I'd drop by. Take your mom somewhere before Vega does. Eat some Greek food. You could come if you want."

"To Athens."

My father nods. "Uh-huh."

"With you and Mom."

"Think about it." Now he really pulls at my shirt. "Come on."

"Where?"

"We're not done, are we?"

I stand up and wipe my nose on one sleeve. "No, there's a couple more."

"So let's stop standing around and get to it. Are they hard?"

"Are you kidding? This next one will kill you."

When we're finished, Dad is too fastidious to shower at Weight World, so we head home. I plug in my iPod this time and up comes Liam Clancy's *The Dutchman*. Unforgiving streets and a coat patched with love.

He gives it thirty seconds, then says, "I thought all you listened to was crap. I didn't know there were things like this." Then he gets on the phone and asks Mom what's for dinner.

"Mac and cheese," he tells me as he closes his phone.

"Mom's mac and cheese is out of this world."

"Then at least go the speed limit. I'm starved."

Not so starved he doesn't stand behind me as I put the car away, signaling left then right then left, so it's parked just the way he likes it.

When we walk in, he heads straight for the shower. Mom's on the phone, and if it's with Vega, I think that's rude. But she looks a little pale as she hangs up.

"What's wrong?" I ask.

"I just talked to Andy's mother. He got stopped because a taillight was burned out. The police smelled alcohol, searched his car, and found marijuana in the glove compartment. He told them it was yours. That you wanted him to hold it for you and he said no, but you must've put it in there, anyway. You didn't, did you?"

I take a deep breath. I look at the stove. "No."

"Ryan."

"Mom, I haven't been around Andy in a long time." I take my hands out of my pockets. Finally I tell her, "He was scared. He probably couldn't think of anything else to say."

"You don't know how badly I want to believe you." She leans against the counter. "I am so tired."

I put my arms around her. The phone she's still holding hits me in the back of the head.

That night Betty asks, "So did she believe you?"

"Took her a minute, but yeah. Then she cried for like ten seconds, had a glass of wine, and I helped her set the table."

"You're not going to get in trouble, are you?"

"With the cops? No way. I wasn't even in the car. Andy was just looking for somebody to blame."

I've got a pile of clean laundry on my dresser, and I'm sorting T-shirts and socks while Betty and I are talking. But I stop when she asks, "Ryan, do you miss Charlotte?"

"Kind of. Do you?"

"I don't know. I think about her. Grandma's got her on her prayer list. If it hadn't been for her, we wouldn't be together."

I put the white T-shirts on top of the other ones. They're so plain compared to my old band tees that they're almost quaint. "My dad was talking in the car on the way home from the gym, and he said sometimes things get to a point where there's just nothing anybody in this world can do."

"We went a lot. We really did what we could. We'd still be there if her dad hadn't said we couldn't."

"Yeah, maybe. Probably."

"Are you tired? You sound tired."

"Kind of. I did the circuit with Dad at the gym, and then I did some more free weights on my own when Rhett showed up."

"Let's go to sleep, then. I'll see you tomorrow."

One of the reasons I like Betty is because she's not fake-nice. She's actually nice.

Four hours later Charlotte shows up at the foot of my bed. Hair in a ponytail, the white shirt, the boots, the pants.

She holds out one hand and says, *"I'm on my way back, Ryan. Come to the hospital. I want you to be there."*

I sit straight up in bed, pulling at the neck of my T-shirt and trying to swallow.

I'm on my way back. I want you to be there.

I get up, splash water on my face, and pull on the nearest pair of pants. Outside the neighborhood is quiet and dark. I get into my mother's black Pathfinder and lock the doors. My heart is beating so hard that I can barely breathe. I tell myself, "Don't go too fast. Don't get pulled over."

At the hospital the striped arm at the entrance to the parking lot is up. A few cars are parked at weird angles, maybe people who rushed to the ER.

When the elevator door opens upstairs, the first thing I see is Monica running at top speed down the hall. Toward Charlotte's room. Which makes me run, too. Makes me grab hold of the doorjamb of 531 to stop myself. Makes me look before going inside. Monica has Charlotte in her arms. I can hear . . . something. Sounds coming from her. From Charlotte. Faint coughing sounds.

I say, "Oh my god."

"Get in here," Monica says. "Hold her up so she can breathe. I was sitting at the desk a minute ago when the monitors went nuts. Don't let her lie flat. I'll be right back."

Charlotte's eyes flutter wildly. Her mouth opens and closes. Nothing that makes any sense comes out, but something does. Something hoarse and gurgly, but a sound. One that she made.

"Wha . . . ?" She has to lick her lips to finish. "What's . . . ?"

I tell her, "You're in the hospital. You've been asleep."

Charlotte's eyes roam. "Who are you?"

"You don't know me," I say.

She turns to me, squints. "Sure I do," she whispers. "You're always with that fat guy Andy."

Just then a nurse I don't know steps between us. "Your parents are on their way, Charlotte."

I say out loud, "Man, they are gonna be so happy."

The nurse turns around and looks at me. "Who are you again?"

TWELVE

Almost the end of June and it's really hot in Monrovia. I get inside where it's air-conditioned before I call my mom. "I'm at the hospital. Thad was doing okay at home, but then he got sick again."

"I just talked to Charlotte's mom. I'd left her a message a long time ago about how glad I was for her and Dr. Silano."

I step back and let some worried-looking people get on the elevator ahead of me. "She prayed every day for two hours, so now she thinks her prayers were answered."

"Well," Mom says, "weren't they?"

"Yeah, but why hers for Charlotte and not yours for Molly?" Before she can say anything, another elevator's doors slide open. "I gotta go. I'll see you later."

Upstairs I stop by room 531 and peek in. Empty. And spooky. Charlotte's curtains are gone and the old ones are back. All those snaps of her are missing and there's a painting of a sailboat where they used to be. Once she was awake, when I came by to see Thad, there was always somebody with her. Lots of somebodies.

Down the hall Thad's curled up in bed watching *The Matrix* again.

I lean in the door. "Hey, man." I look around. Some of his stuff is back—the laptop, the PlayStation paraphernalia.

He struggles to sit up. "You look . . ." Thad searches for the right word. "Competitive."

I glance down at my Nike pants with the lightning bolt down the side. "Don't tell anybody at Aardvark's, but these are from Macy's."

Thad says, "I've got an uncle who buys his suits in the boys' department. I really hope that doesn't happen to me."

"How old are you, again?"

"Eleven."

"You'll grow more. I'm still growing."

"Really?"

"Absolutely."

He holds up a little notebook with a tic-tac-toe grid already drawn on it. We trade the pen, play three games, and tie every time.

Then he asks, "Where's your tunes, anyway?"

"In my backpack."

"I've never seen you without it. You look kind of naked."

"I downloaded some stuff last night."

He tells me, "Charlotte went home a couple of days ago. Didn't she tell you?"

"Betty did."

"She comes back for rehab, though. She's probably here now. So you can find her if you want to."

I sit down on the edge of the bed. "Listen to this. You're not the only one with crazy dreams." I glance toward the door before I say, "I dreamed Charlotte told me she was on her way back from the other side. That's why I was here that night she woke up."

Thad says, "How cool is that?"

"But then she barely knew who I was."

Thad nods. "They never remember what happens in Deadville. You had that dream because you've got the gift."

I just look at him. "What gift is that?"

He scoots closer. "When I was home, I got on the Net and it said sometimes people who have been really sick or in a really bad accident, when they get better they have the gift, so they know stuff."

"Except nothing really bad happened to me."

He tugs at his hat, then holds on like he's afraid it's going to blow off. "Are you kidding? Your sister died, and your friend fell off a horse and almost died. You totally qualify. Anyway, I'm glad I've got the gift 'cause even if I never grow another inch, I'll still be able to see what's going to happen and tell people. Nobody'd call me Emo then."

"So, are you still dreaming?"

"All the time," he whispers. "A couple of days ago, I had this dream and Monica was in it and a kid who fell off his bike and hurt himself. So I told Monica to make sure her little boy wore his helmet all the time. The next day she comes back and says, 'Guess who took a tumble and hit his head?'"

"Thad, a lot of kids fall off their bikes."

"Not in front of Monica's house."

"Well, my dream was right on the money. Charlotte said she was going to wake up and she did."

When Thad yawns, I point to the door. "I'll catch you later, okay?"

"Later today or like tomorrow or when?"

"Probably tomorrow. I'll bring Betty."

Thad waves me back. "We're going to do stuff when I get out of here again, right?"

"Right."

"Betty said we would."

"Then we will."

"Go to the movies, play video games, whatever."

"Sure."

He shakes his head. "Don't say 'Sure' like that. My dad says it like that, and it means 'No.'"

"I promise."

When he holds out his hand, I take it. He looks me right in the eye. His are green with little flecks of black in them. I didn't plan to say anything but I do, anyway. "Where do you think Molly is? I mean is she out there with millions of other souls just waiting to come back again? Or is it all over and she's in some kind of heaven, or is she just a little bit of energy mixed up with a whole lot of energy, or what?"

He doesn't let go of me. "I don't know. They don't tell me that kind of stuff yet."

"They?"

He points up. "The people who run Deadville."

"I'll see you tomorrow for sure."

"Are you going to find Charlotte?"

"I might stop by Rehab."

"Don't let her kiss you or anything. She's really pretty, but Betty's about a thousand times nicer. When Charlotte's dad was taking her home, I asked her if she'd come back and see me, and she said she'd try. That was a big fat lie."

"She only said she'd try."

He shakes his head. "She just thinks I'm some dumb little kid she can say anything to."

I ride the elevator down to Rehab, past the babies in Pediatrics, but not all the way down to where they keep the dead bodies. I know this place—gift shop, bathrooms, Rehab, OR, X-Ray—like I know my own house.

Charlotte is resting between the low bars, the ones patients use when they want to make sure they don't fall down. It looks to me like she's just working on her upper body by doing dips. At Weight World we've got a special machine for that.

I watch her tuck her feet and give up after half a dozen.

"Looking good."

She smiles at me. "Oh, it's you." That turns to a groan as she tries to straighten her arms one last time. "No beach volleyball for me till August," she says.

"I just came by to see Thad. He said you were probably down here."

I watch her bend from side to side. She's inspecting her arms, trying to make her triceps show. "Yeah," she says, "and I'll be glad when I never have to see any part of this friggin' place again. I had to go to graduation in a wheelchair."

"So what? You're gonna be as good as new, right?"

"I had plans, okay? Jill and I were going to Balboa Island."

I ask, "When you do come for rehab, go to see Thad, okay?"

She's looking at her nails. "Thad? I'll try, I guess." She steps out from between the parallel bars, then leans into them to do sissy push-ups. "Can I ask you something, Ryan? I mean I appreciated it and all, but when I was in that coma, why were you here all the time? We barely knew each other. It's just weird. My boyfriend only came once. He said seeing me like that made him cry."

"I guess Derek's a pretty sensitive guy."

She nods, totally serious. The little crease between her eyebrows gets deeper as she says, "Well, it's just a little creepy thinking about you being here night and day and me in bed and all. Did you, like, have a crush on me or something?"

I take a towel off the control panel and fold it a time or two. "No," I say. "Nothing like that."

"I already had a stalker. Did you know that Benny Applewhite? We had to get a restraining order."

"So that's what you think? That I'm a stalker?"

"I don't know what you are. You went way out of your way for nothing."

I watch her wipe her hands, then check the clock.

"Hey, babe."

She hurries to meet Derek. Mr. Sensitive. Charlotte links her arm through his. "We're going shopping."

"Gee," I say. "One little coma, and all your clothes are out of style."

"What?"

"Nothing." But when they're almost to the door, I blurt, "I'm glad you woke up."

She doesn't turn around. "God, me too!"

Just then my cell rings, and I know it's Betty. When I'm in Athens with my folks, will I miss calls like these or will I be glad to be on my own? Who knows? I'm such a beginner.

"Ryan? I'm on my break. It is nuts down here. If I have to make another venti half-caf no-whip Crème Frappuccino, I'll shoot myself."

"Make that two. And can I have it to go in a sippy cup?"

"If I don't pour it down your pants first. Where are you, anyway?"

"At the hospital. I stopped by to see Thad, and he told me Charlotte was in the Rehab room."

"How is she?"

"You know how there are all those mirrors in a gym? She can't keep her eyes off herself."

"Well, good for her." I hear a muffled "In a minute." Then to me, "My manager, all of twelve years old with an MBA in nagging, wants me back on the job. Are you picking me up, or am I just coming straight to your house tonight?"

"Straight to the house if that's okay."

"Where are we going?"

"Anywhere there's beef. My dad can't get enough."

"See you then."

I fold up the phone and tuck it in my pocket. Out in the hall, a little girl with her head bandaged up is pushing a wheelchair all by herself.

I ask her, "Want some help?"

She just shakes her head and tries harder. My sister was like that right up to when she just couldn't be like that anymore.

Hey, Molly. Guess who's happy? I didn't mean to be. It just kind of happened. It doesn't mean I don't love you. But I'm forging ahead. I can't help myself. I was thinking about you this morning and looking for just the right cut. I thought about "Amazing Grace," but bagpipes give me a headache and you hated Judy Collins. So I've got Patty Griffin, who never wrote a happy song in her life until somebody dared her to and she came up with "Burgundy Shoes." So let's slip into those, and see where they take us.

I reach for the Play button and listen all the way down in the elevator, all the way through the lobby, and right out to my mom's car. I get in, roll the windows down, and listen to it again.